NICK CARTER IS IT!

"Nick Carter out-Bonds James Bond."
—*Buffalo Evening News*

"Nick Carter is America's #1 espionage agent."
—*Variety*

"Nick Carter is razor-sharp suspense."
—*King Features*

"Nick Carter is extraordinarily big."
—*Bestsellers*

"Nick Carter has attracted an army of addicted readers . . . the books are fast, have plenty of action and just the right degree of sex . . . Nick Carter is the American James Bond, suave, sophisticated, a killer with both the ladies and the enemy."
—*The New York Times*

FROM THE NICK CARTER
KILLMASTER SERIES

Dedicated to the men of the
Secret Services of the
United States of America

A Killmaster Spy Chiller

NICK CARTER

THE TREASON GAME

CHARTER
NEW YORK

A Division of Charter Communications Inc.
A GROSSET & DUNLAP COMPANY
51 Madison Avenue
New York, New York 10010

First Ace Charter Printing March 1982
Published simultaneously in Canada
Manufactured in the United States of America

THE TREASON GAME

ONE

His American name was Martin Steel. His Russian name was Minya Stalin. That's right, another Stalin. In Russian, Stalin means "steel," so it was predictable that this master Soviet spy would pick the name Martin Steel. Except for one thing. Minya in Russian doesn't mean a damned thing. It's just a name.

I knew a few other things about this spy, this man who was right now in a taxi ahead of me, rolling down Rhode Island Avenue toward Logan Circle. I knew that he was husky, weighing in at about a hundred and eighty pounds. I knew that he was multilingual to a fault, speaking eight languages without a trace of his original accent. He was also clever, was a master of disguises, had killed nine American intelligence agents sent to trail him through his various episodes around the globe, and was up to no damned good here in Washington, D.C.

Unfortunately, I had only a vague idea of what the man really looked like. The eight pictures Hawk had shown me from the files varied so much that I could have been looking at eight different men. But there was something about Minya

Stalins's eyes, something unforgettable.

The yellow and black taxi made a complete sweep of Logan Circle, then shot off down Vermont Avenue. Thomas Circle lay two blocks ahead.

"Stay with it," I told my own taxi driver.

"Mister," the driver said, half turning in the seat, "the meter is almost at fifty bucks. I'm an hour past going off duty, and this is crazy. You sure you . . ."

"I'm sure. Stay with that cab if it takes a month."

He sighed, shrugged, gripped the wheel, and glanced at the meter as it moved past fifty bucks.

I'd picked up Martin Steel at Dulles International Airport almost three hours earlier. I'd recognized him by his swagger, not by his looks. I'd seen motion picture films other agents had taken of the spy—from a distance, of course. That swagger was unmistakably that of Minya Stalin, alias whatever you want to call him at any particular time.

What I didn't know, and what Hawk hadn't told me, was what Minya Stalin, alias Martin Steel, was doing coming back to the U. S. at this particular time. He hadn't been in the States in five years, not since a Secret Service man had put a neat bullet hole in his left buttock.

The taxi made a couple of sweeps around Thomas Circle and headed west on Massachusetts Avenue. Ahead was Scott Circle, then Dupont Circle. Christ, was he heading for our headquarters? I mean the headquarters of AXE, the organization headed by David Hawk, the one that had catapulted me from average American citizen many, many years ago into N3, Killmaster for AXE. If Steel knew of our office on Dupont Circle, he'd know that going there would be instant suicide. He'd be far better off letting me tail him a thousand dollars' worth all around Washington.

But the guy didn't call a halt at Dupont. He made a complete sweep of the circle, past our dark storefront, dropped down to M Street, hung a left, and headed back toward Thomas Circle. My own driver was nodding, as though sleep were his due when he was an hour past quitting time.

The meter neared sixty and the driver seemed to revive. I wasn't worried about the fare, but the truth was I was getting considerably bored with this tailing job. I would have happily taken the driver's place in sleepyland. But Hawk had been explicit about the importance of not losing one Minya Stalin, alias Martin Steel.

"The job may seem beneath you, N3," he'd said as I'd stood in his grimy office at the storefront rear on Dupont. "Maybe it is. I'll tell you only this. Lose the guy and we're in trouble, Nick."

So, I wouldn't lose the guy, even though the night was growing dull and I was catching the sleepies from the taxi driver and didn't have the foggiest idea of why this Martin Steel was so all-fired important on this trip to the States. After all, he'd been here dozens of times before that Secret Service guy nipped his tail a good one.

But Hawk hadn't been jesting. I wouldn't lose Minya Stalin/Martin Steel.

Or so I thought.

With a suddenness that surprised me and woke up my driver, the taxi ahead made a hard swoop to the right and stopped with a squeal of tires and brakes in front of the Holiday Inn on Thomas Circle.

"Go on past," I told my driver. "Make a right on Thirteenth and let me out at the corner."

I paid the bill. Sixty-one dollars, representing three hours of driving time since leaving Dulles International. I remember the fare well because I'd bought my first car—a 1929 Model A Ford convertible—for just four dollars more. And I'd overpaid.

I hustled back down M Street, entered the lobby of the Holiday Inn, and saw that familiar swagger entering the elevator. I waited for Martin Steel to turn, to get a good look at his face, but he didn't turn. He faced the back of the elevator and the doors closed.

At the desk, I saw that he'd registered as Martin Steel. Room 605.

I headed for the elevators, figuring on using an old ploy just in case Steel suspected a tail. I would go up to the seventh floor, walk down to the sixth, get a fix on the location of Room 605, then come back downstairs and wait for his next move.

I strode through the lobby, pushing past a gaggle of people all wearing some kind of conventioneer's badge. I caught the initials on the badge of a red-dressed, attractive woman whose badge was especially prominent, thanks to the ample breast on which it was pinned. ANRA. American Newspaper Reporters' Association.

Great. The Soviet Union's most notorious spy had just waltzed through the cream of American journalists on a spy mission so super secret not even Nick Carter, N3, Killmaster for AXE, had been made privy to it. And not a single cream of American journalism had batted an eyelash.

Anyway, I took the elevator to the seventh floor,

and a flight of stairs down to the sixth, eyeballed Room 605, saw that it was in a small alcove off the main corridor, and took another elevator to the lobby, where I figured to sit out Martin Steel's next move.

His next move was waiting for me when the elevator doors slid open.

He stood there in the lobby, facing me. Behind him were all those American journalists, looking at each other's badges, sipping drinks, gossiping, talking, laughing, swapping juicy jokes that I couldn't hear. I could hear only the tinkling laughter and tinkling ice in their drinks.

And I could hear the roar of my own foolhardiness, my own stupidity in letting this man get the drop on me. In Martin Steel's hand was a pistol that looked every bit as big as a howitzer.

The man grinned. He had a lot of gleaming, white-capped teeth. He also had on dark glasses and some plastic stuff that made his face look puffy and old.

But I was sure it was Martin Steel. Sure it was Minya Stalin.

And the howitzer went off, even as my hand was snaking across my chest on its way to Wilhelmina, my precious, many-notched Luger nestled away in an armpit holster.

The bullet caught me in the fleshy part of my right side. Pain that can never be imagined by the unhurt rumbled through my body. I felt myself slumping and knew that I was going unconscious.

I looked up at my killer and saw the big pistol. It was tracking an invisible point somewhere between my eyes as my head eased slowly toward the floor of the elevator.

I waited for death, wishing it would come soon to erase all that lousy pain. The hand that had been snaking up toward Wilhelmina was clutching at the bloody wound in my right side, trying vainly to stem both blood and pain.

Martin Steel seemed in no hurry to put me out of my misery. His grin, so satanic, so gleeful, flickered across my dulling eyes, briefly taking the place of the big pistol as a dying man's final look at death.

His hand tightened on the trigger and I knew I was a dead man.

I had been unaware of the hush that had followed the first deafening boom of Martin Steel's monstrous hand cannon. I hadn't seen the cream of American journalism behind Steel fade away into hidden recesses of the big lobby. I hadn't heard the cessation of tinkling laughter and tinkling ice.

Through my pain and realization of impending death, I was still hearing that tremendous roar of gunfire.

And maybe a few notes of Gabriel's horn.

I didn't see the flash of red behind Martin Steel, didn't see the shiny white badge on that ample breast. I didn't see anything but that toothy, evil grin and that enormous gun that was about to roar once again and send a quarter-ounce of hot lead through an invisible spot between my eyes.

Then I saw the flash of red that was the lady journalist's dress crash into the back of the Soviet spy. I saw the flash of another kind of red as the spy's thunder gun went off a second time. I saw the bullet gouge a hole into the metal of the elevator above my head.

I didn't hear the roar of that last shot. My world had already gone black.

TWO

Her name was Felicia Starr. American name, of course. She was the cream of the cream of American journalism.

She was the cream of the cream of my life. Without her, I wouldn't have a life.

Felicia was there in the recovery room when I came to. The pain in my side was still great, but the bullet had been removed, leaving no significant or lasting damage, and I wasn't bleeding much anymore. A bit of red seeped through the thick bandage just to keep me aware of how human I was.

"Well, are you going to tell me who you are and who he was and what this is all about?"

She was standing above the bed, her arms folded beneath those ample breasts. She still had on the red dress. The badge was gone, cheating me of a legitimate opportunity to continue to stare at that breast. Although her words had been a bit on the stern side, there was laughter behind them. There was compassion, concern, even a little admiration for the man who'd stood in that elevator and stared down the long barrel of a long, long gun.

I opened my mouth to speak, then realized I had nothing to tell the woman who'd obviously saved my life. My weapons had been taken from me, so somebody in the hospital suspected that I wasn't the average citizen who walked around minding his own business. But I hadn't been carrying identification and, even though I couldn't tell anyone— even Felicia Starr—that I was Nick Carter, Killmaster for AXE, I knew that soon the proper wheels would begin to turn and Hawk would be notified that one of his men had been holed out with a howitzer. Felicia Starr, the cream of American journalism, was sharp enough to know that something big was afoot. She had hung around during the surgery, waiting to be the first to talk to me, looking for that big scoop.

"Who are you?" I asked, by way of diversion. And because I really wanted to know.

She told me her name was Felicia Starr. She worked for the *Washington Times* and had never latched onto a story more important than an Alexandria, Virginia dog show. She smelled a story now, and wasn't about to be diverted. She uncrossed her arms, let those ample breasts hang free, and took out a note pad and pen. I saw that she had dimples and freckles, and long auburn hair. She was as beautiful as she was brave.

"Name, please."

She said "please," but there was no "please" in her voice. There was command.

"Woods Hunter," I said, giving a trick name I'd often used. "I'm a newspaper reporter from Des Moines, Iowa. I'm one of you."

"You're a delegate to the convention?"

"Yep."

Her eyes flickered up and down my sheeted frame. There was doubt written all over her lovely face, but she apparently decided to let it slide. She didn't even ask why I wasn't wearing a badge.

"And who was the man who shot you, who was about to make an even bigger mess in that elevator?"

I hadn't been looking at it that way, but her account of what had been about to happen was disgustingly accurate.

"I don't know," I said, remembering that I really had never seen Martin Steel/Minya Stalin face to face and could only guess that the man with the gun had been the Soviet spy.

"Why did he shoot you? Why was he going to finish you off? People don't go around Washington assassinating reporters from Des Moines, Iowa, you know."

I tried to shrug under the sheet. It pulled on the bandage and hurt like hell.

"Would you believe there's a first time for everything?"

"For most things. Not that. Listen, I saved your skin tonight. I deserve some answers."

"Maybe you ought to tell me about it," I said. "I really didn't get to see what happened. You tell me what happened and I'll give you the answers you deserve."

She pursed her red lips, as if not certain how to take my promise. But she told me.

She and her friends had been laughing and joking and drinking in the hotel lobby. That, I knew. A meeting had just ended and another was to start in twenty minutes. A man suddenly came running down the staircase, pushed through a group of journalists and tourists, and took his stance in front of the closed elevator doors. She saw the man take something from his jacket pocket, but wasn't certain until I arrived that it was a gun. She watched the man, though, even after others had turned back to their previous conversations.

"He stood there like a statue, his feet apart, something in his hand. His back was to me, but I could tell that he wasn't waiting to get on the elevator. He was blocking the exit, as though he intended to catch the next person who got off that elevator. Maybe even attack him, or her."

"And you didn't see the gun?"

"Not then. It was after the doors opened and you were standing there with your mouth open that I saw him raise his hand. I saw the gun, saw the flames spit out the end. I guess I screamed, like the others."

Strange. I hadn't heard any screams. Only that crashing roar of thunder.

"Everyone took off in every conceivable direction," Felicia continued. "I suppose I'd have run too, if I hadn't been so stunned. I was frozen to the spot. I stood there like a dummy, watching you slide down the wall, watching the man with the gun take careful aim at your head."

She stopped, bit her lip. Her eyes showed that compassion again, that concern, that admiration.

"What made you hit him like that?" I asked.

"I don't know. Impulse. I just ran at him like a stupid bull. Even as I ran toward him, I expected him to hear me, to turn around and shoot me. But I kept running and I hit him in the back and the gun went off and you were on the floor and I thought to myself that it was all in vain, that I'd actually caused him to kill you. I didn't know that second bullet missed, not until later."

"What happened then?" I said, my heart starting to pound as I anticipated the answer. I could think only of what Hawk had said if I lost Martin Steel.

"I don't know," she said. "After I hit him, he turned to look at me. He grinned like death, and I fainted. Others told me that he pointed the gun at me for a few seconds, then ran out the door. Somebody called the police, but it was too late. He was gone. Now you know it all. Let's have those answers. I want your real name and occupation. I want his real name and . . ."

The door burst open and two burly cops in uniform dashed into the room. They grabbed Felicia by her arms and started hustling her out of there.

"Mr. Hunter, you promised me . . ."

That was all she got out of her mouth before the cops slammed the door. I lay there, feeling the pain in my side, until one of the cops returned and said he was sorry about the lady getting into my room. It wouldn't happen again, he said. Then, before I could even ask him who the hell *he* was, he was gone.

Pain worked up a good head of steam and I pressed my call button. A male nurse came, asked what I wanted and I said I wanted something for pain. He grinned, left, came back in a few minutes, and gave me a shot. It hurt. A few more minutes, though, and I felt no pain at all. I floated around the room, stroked the sheets, the walls, the ceiling, the cool window.

I only vaguely recalled Hawk coming into the room and standing beside the bed. He shook his head from side to side. And then I konked out.

When I awoke, the light was out, the room quiet. Light from outside filtered through the window and made weird shadows on the ceiling. The pain was seeping back and I thought of pressing the call button for another shot. But it wasn't that bad. I'd weather it out.

I sensed, more than knew, that it was nearing dawn. There was a distinctive roar to the city, as though people were just being made aware that a new day was afoot and were warming up their mechanical monsters—otherwise known as cars, buses, trains, trucks—for another go at the world of commerce and industry.

A click at the door took my attention away from the low roar of the city, from the weird shadows on the ceiling. I waited, expecting to see the male nurse enter with another syringe of pain medication. The door didn't open. Not just then. There was another click, then the squeak of a board. I'd forgotten to ask Felicia which hospital I was in, but it was obviously an old one. And it wasn't a military hospital or there wouldn't have been uniformed cops coming to whisk Felicia away.

The click again. This time, the door began to open slowly. I watched, feeling my heart begin to pound. I felt as though I were back on that elevator again, a helpless victim of a tough superspy with a hand cannon.

The door opened about a foot. A white figure slipped inside and closed the door with a click. I strained to see the face of the man in that white uniform. Was it the male nurse who'd given me my pain shot last night? Was it Martin Steel in yet another disguise?

"What is it?" I said hoarsely. "What do you want?"

The man in white acted swiftly then, as though

the sound of my voice was his cue. He fairly leaped across the room, snatched my pillow from beneath my head, and clamped it over my face.

Strong hands bore down on the pillow. Expert fingers found my mouth and nose through the feathers and pinched hard. I couldn't breathe. The hands and fingers kept kneading the pillow, trying to improve on an already perfect job of smothering. I started to fight against the hands, to tear at the pillow, but the man was too strong.

I gave a leap with my feet and raised my middle off the bed. The pain in my right side made all earlier pain seem inconsequential. But I wasn't getting any air. Soon, there'd be no pain. There'd be no life.

Using every ounce of my strength, I bucked against the man, twisted my whole body—wanting to scream at the new rush of pain—and felt my face come clear of the suffocating pillow. I took in a huge gulp of air, relaxed my body for a split second, then bucked again, harder.

The man was pushed away momentarily, surprised at the strength of his victim. He'd expected an easy kill. Well, he wasn't getting it. Damned if I was going to turn into a professional murder victim.

During the split second that the man had been pushed back from the bed, I was on my feet. I hammered two karate chops at his neck, connecting with the second one. He grunted, gurgled, dropped the pillow, and grabbed his damaged throat. I kicked him in the groin. We both fell, he in the middle of the floor with his hands cupped over his genitals, me back against the bed, breathless and full of pain.

I panted against the bed, willing the pain away and trying to get up enough strength to leap on the guy, with arms and legs working in concert. He rose to his feet before I was ready. I prepared for another assault and was surprised when it didn't come. The man ran for the door, opened it and was down the corridor before I could get my act together. I went to the door, peered out, saw nothing but an empty corridor and an unmanned nurses' station far down the way.

I closed the door and made my way to the bed. I lay panting for a few minutes, collecting my thoughts.

Something was really amiss here. I was certain that Hawk had been in my room last night when I was floating from the drugs the male nurse had given me. I had seen him. I hadn't dreamed it.

Yet, there were no guards outside my room. Some husky man in a white male nurse's uniform had walked in here unchecked and had tried to smother me with my own pillow. There should have been guards to prevent that attack. Any agent whose life had been threatened, as mine was on that elevator, would have been placed under heavy guard. That was standard operating procedure.

Why hadn't Hawk ordered guards for me?

I didn't have an answer for that question and I didn't like the way my mind was trying to make up an answer. There was only one thing for sure.

I wasn't safe in that hospital.

Maybe I wasn't safe anywhere, but everybody has to be somewhere. In my case, it was imperative that I be somewhere else.

Five minutes later I was stumbling off down the street in the Washington dawn. Blood from my bandage was trickling down my right thigh.

I won't even try to describe the pain. Or the growing weakness.

THREE

"My God, Mr. Hunter, what are you doing here? Why aren't you still in the hospital? You're bleeding like a—for the love of God, come inside before you fall over dead."

Felicia Starr was part angry, part frustrated, part perplexed, and a whole lot concerned. I saw that look of admiration in her eyes, and I loved it. But only for a moment, as I was falling through her doorway and passing out in her arms.

She was in a pink nighty and negligee. I was in a white hospital gown and striped robe. Some of those stripes were blood. My right foot, bare, was red and crusted with blood.

The faint didn't last long. I awoke on her bed while she was tightening my hospital bandage to stem the flow of blood. Her lovely mouth was going like sixty and her anger had won out over all the other parts.

I was catching hell. She soon shut up to let me explain.

I'd fled the hospital, I told her, because I'd become convinced that I couldn't trust anyone. I'd walked down Fifth Street Northeast from O Street, found an all-night diner six blocks from the hospital (it was St. Anthony's, I learned), and slip into a booth. A highly curious waitress had served me coffee while I tried to clear my mind of drugs, tried to decide what to do next, tried to decide whom I could trust, if anyone.

I'd concluded that some kind of conspiracy existed, but I couldn't tell Felicia that. I couldn't tell her who I was, couldn't tell her about David Hawk and AXE and the storefront office on Dupont Circle. I just told her that I was in trouble, that I had depended on certain friends, and now knew that those friends couldn't be trusted.

It was true. Just no names were mentioned.

"And so you decided that you could trust me," she said, clucking over me and tucking a clean white cloth beneath the blood-soaked bandage.

"That's about it," I said. "You're my court of last resort.

"Felicia," I said, gazing intently at her eyes, noticing that they were a rich blue, even in the gray dawn light, "you'll just have to accept what I say as fact. I've already brought enough grief on your house . . ."

"Apartment," she interrupted.

"Apartment," I echoed. "I can't tell you everything that's happening or your house—your apartment—would know the ultimate grief. Just help me, don't ask questions, and be patient. Trust me. You'll know it all in time."

She sat back after having staunched the blood flow, though not the pain. "So, you sat in that diner, decided that your friends couldn't be trusted and came to me. How did you find me?"

She didn't believe that I'd called her newspaper and gotten her address. She was right in not believing it. No newspaper in its right mind would give out addresses on employees to anonymous callers. I couldn't tell Felicia that I'd tapped into AXE's computer bank and gotten her address through the Freedom of Information Act. Such a revelation would have brought her close to the truth and we'd agreed that she'd wait for the truth.

Felicia also didn't believe that I'd walked the twenty-seven blocks from that diner to her apartment near Embassy Row, near the Gallery of Modern Art. But I had no money and, even if I had, no taxi driver would have stopped for such a wobbly, bloody apparition. So, I'd walked that twenty-seven blocks. I was paying for it. The pain in my side was so great that I wanted to die.

"The point now," I said, "is that I can't stay here. By now, my so-called friends have learned how I got your address and will be on my trail. I'm depending on you to get me away from here, to some safe place where I can recuperate and decide what to do next."

She looked at me for a long time. Gray light danced on her freckled cheeks and made her eyes a darker blue.

"Why should I go to all that trouble?" she asked. "Even if I could."

"Because it's your fault that I'm not a bloody mess on the back wall of an elevator. You saved my life. It's up to you to keep me alive. I'm your responsibility."

"In that case," she said, almost smiling, "you'd better give me a better name than Woods Hunter to go on."

"Pick a name," I said.

"Forest Creature fits you better right now."

"I can live with that," I replied. "Just so I live."

She sighed and shrugged. Heavy breasts rose and fell, delightfully. "All right, Forest. I just happen to have the place for your sanctuary. A friend has a cottage on the Patuxent River up near Laurel, Maryland. It can't be traced to me because the friend—well, we're no longer such close friends, and he's in Europe now with his new playmate, and I think that's enough of that story. The point is, I have a key and carte blanche use of the cottage. Do you feel up to traveling now?"

"No, but I have no choice." I was ready to ask for the key to the cottage and directions for how to get there, but a warning bell rang deep in the back of my mind. "I'd like to know more about this friend," I said. "You don't have to tell me about your involvement, but I need to know who he is, what he is, just in case . . ."

She laughed. "Just in case he's tied in with the traitors? Don't worry. Lance Huntington could probably buy and sell all the traitors in both Russia and the U. S."

I'd heard of him. International playboy and womanizer. Leader extraordinaire of the jet set. Former Vietnam fighter pilot whose family not only could have paid to keep him out of the war, but could have bought Vietnam, North and South alike.

Felicia continued, "Who else do you know who keeps a Learjet at Washington National Airport for local travel and one in a hangar in London for continental hops? Who else do you know who charters a whole TWA superjet when he wants to visit one or the other of his Learjets? Who else do you know . . ."

"I've got the picture," I said, a little curious as to why this intelligent and lovely girl had been one of this notorious jerk's playmates. "Just give me the key and some directions. You stay here."

She shook her head. That special look returned to her eyes. "You're a tough bird, Woods, but not that tough. I take you in my car or it's no go."

I thought of what must be happening behind the scenes to have let that fiasco go down in the hospital before dawn. I caught a premonition of this lovely lady, me and the car going up in a ball of very loud flame and debris. I almost told her the truth of what she was up against.

"The key and the directions, fine lady. You're already in enough jeopardy."

She reluctantly let me have my way. I gave myself a twenty-minute rest on her bed and left as I'd come, in bloody robe and gown. I left instructions for her to go about her job as usual. I'd be in touch when I felt the time was right. I did relent on the money angle, though, letting her advance me cab fare. Providing, of course, I could find a cabbie who'd pick me up.

Several did. I wove about the city for an hour, taking one cab after another, until I felt safe to take a bus up to Langley Park. From there, I caught a hitch with a young guy in a pickup truck, got off at a busy intersection in Montpelier, took another bus to Laurel, and walked to the cottage, up along the riverbank.

I was counting heavily on what agents call the "unbelievability factor." People would talk about the man in the bloody hospital garb, but few would believe them.

The cottage was perfect in some respects, a trap

in others. It was on a high embankment above the river, with only one entrance and exit. The rear of the cottage was a screened-in porch on stilts high above the water. Once inside, there was no back way out, except through a screen and into the murky waters below. But I didn't count on being found and trapped.

The interior of the cottage was ultra modern and redolent of wealth. The modern kitchen was well stocked with all the necessities, especially Scotch. I had no cigarettes—my special Turkish blend with my initials in gold on them—but there were some Dorals in a drawer and I puffed on them as I paced the cottage and tried to figure out what was happening to me.

In my pacing, I found a closet full of Lance Huntington's clothing. I put on a swanky sports outfit of turtleneck velour sweater, white duck trousers and silk scarf—all Pierre Cardin—and calfskin Gucci loafers over silk socks. I burned the hospital outfit in the incinerator. A first-aid kit in the main bathroom provided an adequate new bandage and, with a couple of belts of twelve-year-old Scotch, I didn't feel any more pain than I could handle.

I sat down to think.

Point one, somebody tipped Martin Steel/ Minya Stalin that he was being followed. He didn't tumble to me. If he'd known someone was following him in a taxi, he'd not have seen who it was. The man who stood at that elevator door with that hand cannon knew who to expect. He probably had at least eight pictures of me, all of them looking exactly like Nick Carter. I don't pretend to be a master of disguise.

Point two, somebody tipped that male nurse, or nurse imposter, that I was in that room, wounded and presumably helpless.

Point three, those two cops who came and whisked Felicia out of my room were not Washington cops. They had no identifying insignia on their uniforms. They were special forces people sent there by . . . whom?

Point four, if Hawk was in my room—and I knew he was—why did he leave me there without guards? Why didn't he have me transferred to Bethesda Naval, or to some quiet clinic where we have our own people on duty?

There were other points, most of them minor. The main thing was that all the points added up to one thing:

Somebody in AXE, or somebody who knew of AXE's operations, was a traitor.

At the moment, the finger of suspicion pointed to the one man I had always known I could trust above all others, above all else.

That man was David Hawk, my boss.

In years past, David Hawk had rescued me, or caused me to be rescued, from all manner of dire conditions. He'd commandeered sophisticated military hardware, including an aircraft carrier, to pluck me from death-threatening situations. Sometimes he'd come personally to various points of the globe to aid in my rescue; sometimes he'd relied on trusted friends, aides, and other agents.

But at the heart of every daring rescue had been the heart of David Hawk. I was his best agent. There were times when I considered myself his best friend.

It was impossible for him to betray me. And yet. . . .

Such thoughts rambled and festered in my brain for the next four days. I went through a series of fevers and came out with the same troubling thought:

David Hawk had betrayed Nick Carter.

Felicia Starr kept her word, though, and never came near the cottage. She didn't call or send a messenger. I was quite alone with my monstrous thoughts. And no one, I was certain, knew where I was. For the moment, I was safe from Martin Steel. And from Hawk.

On the fifth day, I left the cottage wearing another hotshot sports outfit that smacked of Cardin, smelled of Cardin, and felt of Cardin. I took several buses all the way up to Rockville and went to a public phone booth on the sidewalk and called the special number. I gave my own code to the radioman, demanded to speak to the man in charge and waited until Hawk came on the scrambler.

"Where the hell are you?" he demanded. "Where the hell have you been?"

"Never mind all that," I said in a tone that I'd never used with my boss before. "I'll ask the questions. You give the answers."

I had my wristwatch out on the little metal change counter and was watching the sweep of the second hand.

"Nick, are you all right?" His voice sounded less harsh, more tentative.

"I'm fine. Physically. I want to know why you didn't move me from St. Anthony's Hospital, or at least put on some guards."

There was a pause. "Would you mind telling me what the hell you're talking about?"

I hung up and went down the street to another pay phone. My watch had warned me that the computer was on the verge of tracing my location. When Hawk was on the line again, I went over all that had happened, from the moment Martin Steel had shot me, to the moment Hawk came to see me in the hospital, to the moment the man in white tried to turn off my lights with the pillow. I left out Felicia Starr's help, her very existence. Then, I hung up and went to yet another phone, and got Hawk on the line.

"N3," he said with his usual authoritarian tone, "this is all news to me. I read of a shooting of an unidentified man at the Holiday Inn, but didn't connect it to you. I never got word that you were at St. Anthony's Hospital. I only know that you failed to report in at the prescribed time and presumed that you'd run into some trouble with our friend from over the ocean. Your whole story is brand new to me."

"That's bullshit," I snarled into the phone just before I hung up the receiver. I went to a fourth phone, got Hawk again and continued as though there'd been no interruption. "You were in my room. I saw you standing above the bed. Two cops barged in and took away a visitor I had."

"N3, you've cracked up. I was never at St. Anthony's. I don't know anything about two cops taking any visitor. By the way, who was the visitor?"

"Never mind. Are you trying to tell me that you didn't come to my room when I was doped up with painkiller?"

"You're not making sense. You're . . ."

I hung up and went to a hotel lobby and called from another phone. Hawk finished his sentence.

"You're making up some crazy story to hide the fact that you've lost our friend from across the ocean. Isn't that it?"

"I got a bullet hole in my side that says I'm not making up anything," I growled. The effort of leaving the cottage and coming all the way to Rockville was making the damned thing begin to hurt again. There was even a little blood seeping through the black stitches. "If anyone is making up things, it's . . ."

I heard the distant whistling and knew that the computer had a fix on my location. I hung up and took another bus all the way up to Frederick. I'd have gone to Baltimore, but there wasn't a bus for an hour and I wanted this business cleared up before anything else.

"I won't make any accusations," I told Hawk when he was on the line again, "but something is wrong. Somebody is telling the enemy all my moves, helping him to eliminate me. And . . ."

"And you suspect it's me," Hawk said. He always could read my mind.

"I didn't say that. But you sent me out to chase a spy, didn't tell me any details as to why he's here, threatened me with all sorts of agony if I lost him, and then the guy nailed me to the cross once and tried to do it again. He has inside information. He *has* to have it. And I have to know where he's getting it."

I went to yet another phone to continue.

"I'm going to find out where he's getting it and then I'm going to blow the bastard to Kingdom come and go after his sources. If you're involved, you'll get the same treatment as any other traitor."

Hawk sighed. It was a sigh of exasperation, the kind a father gives out when he's dealing with an unruly and very dumb child.

"If I tell you why our friend is here, would that help?"

"It sure as hell wouldn't hurt."

He told me, through about three more phones, but I wasn't sure if he was telling me the truth:

Martin Steel/Minya Stalin had come to the U. S. in advance of a Soviet nuclear inspection team. The team was due in one week and it would check out, under United Nations guidelines, a new missile site the U. S. was building in Utah and Nevada. In a reciprocal action, a U. S. inspection team would leave for Russia in a week to check out a new missile site in the Urals.

Everything had been worked out by the diplomats. The only fly in the ointment was that the Russians had sent Minya Stalin, and UN officials had specifically spelled out that there was to be no spying activity prior to or during the two inspection tours. The President had asked Hawk to find out why Minya Stalin was coming at this time. If his mission concerned the missile inspections, he was to be apprehended and deported immediately.

"The missile inspections are all-important," Hawk concluded. "They're very sensitive operations. Nothing—I repeat—nothing can go wrong. The success of the inspections has a vital bearing on future SALT talks. It has a direct bearing on the future of the free world, of the entire planet. One wrong move and some nervous finger will start pushing buttons. Once that happens, no force on earth can halt a planetwide devastation by the most powerful and most sophisticated missiles and nuclear warheads ever devised."

"And my losing Martin Steel represents a wrong move?"

"Precisely. Now you have to find him, apprehend him, and I'll arrange for his quiet deportation."

"Do you have a fix on his location?"

"None whatsoever."

I still didn't trust Hawk. There was something missing from his story. He had been in that hospital room, yet he denied even knowing that I was there. And he wouldn't admit that he was lying. I decided to test him.

"My next step, then, is to get out to those missile sites and see if our friend is . . ."

"No!"

It was a bark and a belch and a bellow and a profane epithet all in one.

"Why not?"

"You're to stay strictly away from those sites. We can't have any involvement there. The inspection teams are preparing their groundwork on both sides. It's all going smoothly. It's a very, very sensitive . . ."

"I have to do what I have to do," I said and rang off for the last time.

Seven buses and three hours later, I was walking down the narrow lane alongside the Patuxent River. The cottage was just ahead and I was so weary that all I could think of was that soft bed with its silk sheets. And all that lovely Scotch and gourmet food that Lance Huntington was so fond of.

As preoccupied as I was with comfort, drink and food, I took time to study the path along the river. It was an old habit when returning to a sanctuary I'd left temporarily. I saw what I was hoping not to see.

There, in the soft dirt alongside the path, were fresh footprints. Several men, all wearing dress shoes, had been on this path and were probably in the cottage waiting for me. I checked farther along and, sure enough, there were more footprints. Some pointed toward the cottage, some pointed away, indicating that they'd come and gone.

Maybe.

I retraced my steps and found a shallow part in the river. I went across on stones, keeping out of the water, and moved down through the brush on the other side until I was opposite the cottage. I hunkered down to watch. An hour passed and nothing happened. I was just preparing to leave my surveillance post when it happened.

The whole cottage exploded in a massive ball of fire. Flaming debris shot high into the air and landed in the river, sizzling like steak on a barbecue pit.

They'd left a time bomb, set to go off when I was back in the cottage, when I was in there gorging myself on Lance Huntington's marvelous food and swilling down his lovely Scotch.

Somebody was playing an awfully rough game with me. I was used to that. But now I had a new name to add to my list of prime suspects:

Felicia Starr. She was the only one who knew

about the cottage, knew that I was in it.

The missile sites would have to wait. Martin Steel would have to wait. The traitor—or traitors —were right here in the Washington area. I'd find them. As for deportation, I would deport them all right. Not to another country, though.

I'd deport them to hell.

FOUR

For years I've had an apartment on O Street, not too far from Dupont Circle. Not even Hawk knows about it. It was dark when I got there. Even though I was convinced that no one knew of the place, I entered cautiously, checking for trip-wires, making certain all my security measures were in place—tiny hairs shoved into crevices around the door, Scotch tape across the spot where the knob turns, things like that. The apartment was clean.

I took a short nap, ate some dry cereal I kept around the place, then replenished my weapon supply. I snuggled a new Pierre, one of my lethal gas bombs, into a new lambskin pouch behind my testicles. I had a few non-lethal Pierres loaded with an incapacitating nerve gas, but this time I wouldn't use them. I was going in for the big kill.

Next came a brand new Wilhelmina, *sans* notches, and a new armpit holster. I loaded the Luger with its 16-count clip of 9mm slugs and slipped two more rounds into my jacket pocket—the Cardin jacket pocket that Felicia's friend, Lance Huntington, had provided me before all his goodies went up in a ball of flame and destruction.

For some strange reason, the new Wilhelmina

and holster didn't feel just right snuggled up there in my armpit. There was a new feeling and a new smell to the weapon and its holster. I thought of going back to St. Anthony's Hospital to nose around for the confiscated Luger and other weapons. But I quickly discarded that idea.

I strapped a new sheath to my forearm and slid in a new Hugo, my trusty and beloved and very lethal stiletto. It also felt strange and new. The sheath had a trigger device that worked from the muscles of my forearm. One twitch of that muscle and the shiny, needle-pointed weapon snapped quickly and easily into my right hand. I tried it out just to get my rhythm back, and realized that I'd never lost the rhythm. Like riding a bicycle, I suppose.

Then, again a walking arsenal, I went back to the streets. It was past two in the morning, but I wasn't worried about rankling any feelings with my late calls. I found a phone booth on New Hampshire Avenue and called Felicia. She answered in a voice that was thick with sleep—and sexuality. I was almost sorry that I couldn't respond in kind.

"All right, who'd you send out to blow my parts apart?"

She either didn't know what the hell I was talking about or she was as good at playing games as Hawk was. I listened to a plethora of "who's" and "what's" and "huhs" and then told her about the cottage and the interesting display of pyrotechnics.

"Oh my God, Lance will kill me when he gets back from Europe," she said.

"I'll beat him to it," I said, "unless I get some clear answers. Who did you tell I was out there?"

"No one," she snapped. "Good Lord, Woods,

do you think I'm one of *them?*"

"I don't know who you are, lady," I barked. "All I know is that you're the only one who knew I was out at that cottage. You had to tell someone. Who was it?"

"Only my boss," she said. "I told him I was onto what promised to be a really hot story and that I had the subject—you—hidden away. I didn't say where."

"Question one," I said. "Who is your boss? Question two. Does this boss know about your former arrangement with your friend, Lance Huntington, who's supposed to be in Europe?"

She gave me her boss's name. It was Jordan Alman, an associate editor of the *Washington Times.* As for his knowledge of her affairs, yes, he knew of Lance Huntington, of his various cottages and apartments, even of his two Learjets, one in Washington, one in London.

"If he knew pretty boy Lance," I said caustically, "he not only knew of the cottage, he probably knows what color silk shorts the guy wears. Save me some time and tell me where Jordan Alman lives."

"Oh no, you're not going to get me in trouble by calling him up in the middle of the night."

"I won't call him," I said. "I promise."

She told me where he lived. Naive kid. She should have known that I'd live up to my promise and not call her boss, that I would pass up the call and go directly to his house. I wasn't pleasant when I said goodbye. I still didn't trust her. I wanted to, almost as much as I wanted to trust Hawk.

Alman lived, predictably, in a rambling old Victorian up in Silver Spring. By now, I wasn't depending on buses and taxis. I'd taken my TR7 sports coupe out of mothballs and was saving wear and tear on my weary body and nerves.

I entered the house through a rear window above a porch roof. Jordan and his wife had separate bedrooms, which helped. Once I'd figured out the lay of the house, checking points of hasty egress, I went in and woke him up. His eyes popped open and saw the bit round hole in the end of Wilhelmina.

"What in the . . ."

He started to rise, but I pressed the Luger's barrel against his forehead and pushed him back into the pillow.

"Just one piece of information," I snarled. "Who did you tell about Felicia Starr's subject for a really hot story? Don't screw around with a bunch of questions. Just give me the answer I want."

He was a savvy guy. Most people are when there's a gun making a dent in their forehead and the man behind the gun is growling through his nose, hinting that he's not there for nonsense.

"I didn't tell anyone until today at lunch," he said. He looked at his watch. "*Yesterday* at lunch," he corrected.

"And who was that?"

"Peter Wilding," he said. "He's . . ."

"I know who he is. He's Senator Lou Barker's administrative assistant. And Senator Barker is on the Senate Nuclear Energy Committee. Why did you tell Peter Wilding about Felicia's mystery guest?"

He shifted uncomfortably on the bed. "Would you mind moving that thing back an inch or so? I have to scratch my backside and I'm afraid it'll go off."

I eased off and let him scratch his ass.

"It was inadvertent," he said. "Peter was telling me about something he'd heard up on the Hill. Something about a Russian spy who came to the U. S. a few days ago and may have killed, or tried to kill an American agent in a Holiday Inn elevator. I remembered Felicia's story and figured her subject was that agent, that he hadn't been killed."

"So, in an innocent chit-chat, you told him about Felicia and her story, then happened to mention that she probably had her subject, the agent, hidden away in Lance Huntington's cottage up on the Patuxent. Is that about the size of it?"

"That's it exactly. I didn't see any harm . . ."

"Most people see no harm in gossip," I said, believing the man's innocent story. "This time, it almost got me blown to bits. As it is, you have some explaining to do to old Lance when he gets back from Europe. Just do me one favor. Forget I was here. Forget Felicia's story. Don't gossip. If my trail leads back to you, Mr. Alman, I'll do more than make a little red spot in the middle of your forehead. I'll plaster your brains all over this room."

I left before he could respond. I knew he would be on the phone as soon as I left, so I yanked out all the wiring I could find and then slipped out the way I'd come in. The TR7 was ready to purr and travel.

I skipped the next obvious step. I could have gone to Peter Wilding and learned that he mentioned Jordan Alman's curious story to his boss. I went directly to the boss, to the College Park home of Senator Lou Barker.

The senator was a fat man who lived in a fat house. His fat wife, fortunately, was off on a visit, so I had the fat but important legislator all to myself. Except for a butler who was snoring so loudly that he actually covered my footfalls. The senator awoke to the same unholy vision Jordan Alman has seen.

"Who the hell are you? What the hell do you want?"

"I'm the sandman," I said, grinning over the top of Wilhelmina. "I came to listen to a bedtime story."

I told him all I wanted him to know, then asked whom he'd told Peter Wilding's gossipy report about his luncheon conversation with the associate editor of the *Times*.

"After you tell me that," I added, "I have some other questions about an incident at the Holiday Inn on Thomas Circle, and in St. Anthony's Hospital about dawn a few days ago."

He started the innocent routine, but his little pig's eyes in all that fat told me that he was lying through his teeth. I decided on another approach. I got the senator out of bed, marched him down to the den where we couldn't hear the butler's snores, and made him take off his pajamas. He sat like a flabby Buddha in his favorite chair, red from embarrassment.

The whole gambit was to make him embarrassed, to reduce him in stature, at least in his own eyes, and make him amenable to coercion. I had no intentions of using physical torture, although I figured the man for a coward who would spill everything he knew at the first sign of pain.

I hadn't figured on the senator's massive ego. In a few minutes, he was over his embarrassment at being naked in front of an armed stranger. He became as pompous and egomaniacal as if he were fully dressed and badgering a weaker opponent in a floor battle in the Senate chamber. I let him bluster for a while.

"This is not the American way. You can't do these things in America. I'll see to it personally that you are convicted and sent to prison for the rest of your natural life. Law and order and civilization cannot tolerate bullies like you and . . ."

And so on.

He ran down after thirty minutes, but only because it was late and he was tired and thirsty. I'd denied a half-dozen requests for a Scotch and water. I wanted the man sober and thirsty and lucid. But I had to get him on track soon. It was coming up on dawn again. The butler would soon finish his snoring and start making the senator's morning coffee. And, from the looks of the senator, his usual breakfast feast.

I tried another ploy, convinced that I was right on target.

"Senator, I happen to know that you've been feeding the Russians what you consider harmless information for specific sums of money. A retainer, if you will. I happen to know that your bank accounts in a dozen banks are growing fatter than you are, and it's not all from kickbacks from contractors. When it comes to prison terms, yours will outlast mine if the Russians let you live that long."

I had only a hunch that the man was on the Soviet payroll. I had no idea of any bank accounts. But the ploy hit paydirt as if I'd done a lot of home-work on this man. I had done a little. The Russians seemed to know much more than they should of our entire nuclear program. Someone on the Nu-clear Energy Committee in the Senate or the House was on the take. Senator Lou Barker was as good a suspect as anyone.

"You have no proof of any of that," he barked. There wasn't much bite in his bark.

"Enough to put the Justice Department on the right trail," I said coolly.

That did it. He sagged in his chair. Folds of fat seemed to melt down into his lap. The room was chilly, but the fat body was covered with a sheen of sweat. Yet, his old ego was still working. He grinned slyly and glanced around the room.

"Even if you have all this on tape," he said, "you've already broken so many laws that any-thing said here will not be admissable in a court of law. Not even the Justice Department people will listen to a maniac who got his information through coercion, threats, a gun. If you leave now, my friend, this will all be forgotten. If you pursue this line, you will be . . ."

I screwed a silencer onto Wilhelmina and pulled the trigger. The hot slug whizzed past the senator's balding head and lodged with a plunk in his rich, plastered, tapestried wall. The sheen of sweat be-came a series of rivers.

"The next shot will be aimed quite a bit lower," I said. "Your friends seem to prefer gut shots and head shots. I'll use their technique. First, the gut for pain, then, after a suitable interval of agony, I'll go for the spot between the eyes. Imagine, if you will, the lion's share of your skull and brains plastered all over that fine wall behind you."

He glanced at the wall behind him, at the ugly hole in his expensive tapestry. His whole body shuddered. Sweat came in torrents now, not even following the folds and wrinkles.

"I get a little money," he said, wringing his hands together and studying me with a wild look in those little pig eyes. "I get it for practically nothing. I pass along things that could be picked up in any library. And I don't deal with them directly. There are go-betweens, several of them. There's nothing wrong in that."

"If that's the way your conscience sees it," I said, moving Wilhelmina from his head to his stomach, "who am I to argue. Give me the names of your go-betweens."

I could hardly believe my good luck. With one small demonstration of force, and a lot of suggestion, I'd scared this egomaniac into spilling the fact that he was, indeed, a traitor to the America he professed to love. I remembered his own words: "This is not the American way. You can't do these things in America."

Christ almighty, if this man continued to do the things he was doing, believing them to be innocent, there would be no America. There would be just one massive, planetwide Russia.

"I can't give you names," he protested, still wringing his hands, looking around the room for deliverance from the mess he was in. "I can't . . ."

I squeezed off another shot. This time, the slug laced a red track along his fat left thigh and thudded into the velvet upholstery of the lush chair. He screamed, leaped up, saw that I'd moved the Luger up toward his head, and sagged back into the chair. His pudgy hands clung to the long, shallow wound on his thick thigh, as though to keep all his insides from spilling out, or to catch the precious blood and put it back when I was gone. He was wailing deep in his throat, and he was trembling all over.

"Names," I said. "I want them all. If you even *know* a Russian, I want his name too. You can tell me at your ease, or you can tell me through your agony as your guts try to spit out the next bullet that comes from this gun."

He leaned forward. There was already great agony in him, on his fat face, along his superficially-wounded thigh.

"Who are you?" His voice was a whisper, a plea, a hoarse croak of terror.

I rattled off a bunch of nonsense names, the way I'd done with Felicia. His eyes flitted about as his mind tried to recall if he'd heard those names before.

"It doesn't matter who I am," I said, saving his mind some trouble. "The names I want to hear are the names of the people to whom you fed information, no matter how innocent, no matter how many libraries the information is in. You have three seconds to start naming names before your guts feel the sting of this little toy pistol."

There were four names. Allen Pierson. Donald Stanton. Leland Hutchings. John Pesco.

Pierson was a minor light in the very Justice Department I'd threatened to expose the senator to. A lawyer, a clever, ambitious, money-grubbing slicker from Indianapolis. He was probably the man who made the ultimate contact with the Russians.

The other three men were far too important to take such a large risk.

Donald Stanton was very high-placed, a special envoy between the Atomic Energy Commission and the President. He had information on America's nuclear programs that not even Hawk—and in some cases the President himself—possessed. But his association with the new missile program was possibly trivial at this point.

Leland Hutchings was another well-placed contact. As administrative assistant to Senator Hugh Longley, chief of the Nuclear Energy Committee in the Senate, he was in a prime spot to gather data that was definitely not in libraries, that not even Senator Barker was privy to.

But John Pesco was perhaps the biggest toad of all as it pertained to the current missile program. A former White House chief of staff, he'd been made the chief deputy to Charles Ajax, the administrative head of the missile program. I'd met Pesco at a Washington party, but had seen only newspaper photos of Charles Ajax. Ajax, it would seem from the senator's story, was clean, unaware that his chief deputy was on the take. But I'd have to find that out for myself. I trusted no one at this point.

Unless the senator was lying through his teeth I'd struck the mother lode of a vein of treason that carried the nation's lifeblood down the wrong channels. From the look of terror in Senator Lou Barker's beady eyes, I knew the man wasn't lying. If his mother had been a go-between feeding data from official sources to the Russians, the senator would have given me her name, address, phone number, hair color, and Social Security number. He was that much of a coward.

The big question in my mind now was what to do with the information this coward had given me. Well, actually, information that I'd kind of taken from him.

Did I take the info to Hawk and trust him to do the weeding out? Ordinarily, I would do just that. But I couldn't forget that night when Hawk stood beside my bed in St. Anthony's Hospital. I couldn't forget the man in white and the pillow that had almost put out my lights. I couldn't forget Hawk's obvious lies, denying that he knew I was even in the damned hospital.

It was just possible that Hawk was lying to keep me from knowing something of such vital security to the nation that to divulge it would have been disastrous. I doubted that.

Hawk had lied. Hawk had perhaps inadvertently given the Russians a chance to finish me off. National security or not, there was no excuse for it.

No, I wouldn't go to Hawk. I wouldn't even call him and tell him about my meeting with the senator.

And that led to another problem. What was I going to do with Senator Lou Barker and his sweaty body and cowardly mouth? What was I to do with Allen Pierson and Donald Stanton and Leland Hutchings and John Pesco?

The senator had been right about one thing. If I took my knowledge to the Justice Department, the legal eagles would toss it all out the window because of technicalities. He'd given the information under stress. I'd broken into the man's house and held him at gunpoint. I'd violated his civil rights.

This is not a complaint about the American system. It's a good system. Civil rights must be protected. But not, I decided, at the risk of the life of the nation. In times of war, civil rights of known traitors are ignored or set aside. Innocent people suffer in the interest of national security.

People got all jacked out of shape when Senator Barry Goldwater, running for President, said that extremism in the defense of liberty is no vice. Goldwater had been merely paraphrasing the comments of our forefathers, men like Patrick Henry and Benjamin Franklin and George Washington. And Nathan Hale.

Okay, so much for philosophical musings. I had a nasty problem on my hands here. The minute I left this house, even with the phone wires ripped out, Senator Lou Barker would be in touch with the four men he had named. And a lot of other names. He'd play the injured party and sic the Justice Department on me. The tangled web that would then be woven would be too complex and too massive to undo. It would be a Gordian knot that no sword could sever, no hands untie.

I had no interest in harming innocent people, even in the defense of our nation, but the senator was, by his own admission, not an innocent man. He was on the Russian payroll. As for that crap about feeding them info available in any library, what about the story he'd learned from Peter Wilding through Jordan Alman? The one about Felicia Starr being on a hot story and having her "subject" hidden away in a former lover's cottage?

His divulging of that story nearly led to my demise. And how much of his and his associates' information had led Martin Steel to that elevator door with a hand cannon in his hand? What had he to do with the man in white who came to smother

·me with my own pillow?

There was already a tangled web, a Gordian knot, in the works, and this fat man whom people had trusted was one of the weavers, one of the knot-tiers.

It was not possible to leave him in a position to make that web any more complicated.

I made up my mind as to what I'd do. The pain in my side hardly reflected trouble from the bullet wound Martin Steel had given me. It came from a soul-stirring reaction to my decision.

"Thank you, Senator," I said, rising, still aiming Wilhelmina at his round head. "I'm sorry to have caused you so much trouble and embarrassment. Believe me, your troubles are now over as far as I'm concerned."

His last words were:

"Who are you?"

The hot pellet of lead spat from the muzzle of Wilhelmina's barrel with little more than a whisper. It whizzed through the silencer and crossed the little bit of space between the Luger and the senator's head.

I saw the large red hole, saw the sickening mass of brains and bone and hair on the chair's velvet back, saw the senator's beady eyes roll wildly and then close.

Before I left, I made a flying trip to the senator's downstairs bathroom and heaved up everything I'd eaten in the past twenty-four hours.

FIVE

There are certain things that man is incapable of refusing to do. One of them is flying in the face of danger. This phenomenon often occurs when a man is feeling depressed or guilty. I felt like hell after killing Senator Lou Barker. Guilty *and* depressed.

That's why I couldn't resist going past my regular apartment on my way back into the city from the senator's fat house. I knew Hawk would have it under surveillance, but my own ego was sufficient to make me think I could slip through that surveillance.

I was wrong. Ego trips rarely prove fruitful.

I was no further than a block past the apartment when I spotted the small red Jaguar that is the homebase favorite of N6, the AXE agent who will take my place in the organization's Killmaster ranks when some Martin Steel finally hits the right spot on my body.

Tired as I was, and as sore as my side had become, I had to shake N6. No easy task. He knew that my slate gray TR7 was my homebase favorite, although I rarely used it, as I rarely used my secret apartment.

The problem then, was to get from Point A (my regular apartment) to Point B (my secret apartment) without letting Tangent 1 (the agent known only to me as N6) know where Tangent 2 (me) was going. The tail-shaking trip used up a lot of Washington asphalt and nearly got us both killed at a number of busy circles and intersections. The Jag, with N6 at the controls, was not only speedier and more powerful, it was unshakable. I finally went for a dangerous ploy.

I skidded the TR7 to a stop in front of the Holiday Inn at Thomas Circle, abandoned it, ran inside, punched the elevator button and went up to the seventh floor. I walked back down to the sixth, went to the little alcove outside Room 605, using a plastic credit card to get inside and closed the door with hardly a click.

Dawn light came through the window. The drapes were slightly open. I surveyed the room, saw that the bed was made, as I suspected it would be, and checked the bathroom and closet. The room was empty. I had guessed correctly: Martin Steel had probably reserved the room for several days. Since that altercation on the elevator, he would not be using the room, or even the same hotel.

Through the window, I watched as N6 came back outside and sniffed around my TR7. He made a call on his radio and, pretty soon, a whole raft of agents were on the scene. I saw Hawk's big black limousine roll up across the street. He got out, cigar clenched in his teeth, and marched across to the TR7. His eyes swept the windows of the hotel, but I knew what he was thinking. Nick Carter, he was convinced, had gone out the back way and was right now high-tailing it out of the area in a taxi.

The main danger to the ploy was that Martin Steel or one of his cohorts could have been in Room 605. They weren't here now, but the danger remained. They could return at any moment.

An hour later, the street below was clear. A tow truck came and removed my little TR7. I knew I would find it someday at the city pound. That day would have to wait.

I sat on the killer's bed and planned my next step.

I had killed a United States senator. In any city in the world, that would be big news. In an hour, Tom Brokaw on the Today Show would be telling us all about it.

The main problem was that the world would see Senator Lou Barker as the innocent victim of some hideous monster with a gun. Another political assassination.

I decided my only alternative there was to call Felicia Starr, give her the details (minus the names the senator had given me), and hope her newspaper would print the other side of the story.

As for the others—Allen Pierson, Donald Stanton, Leland Hutchings and John Pesco—there was nothing for it but to line them up like beerbottles on a shelf and put an end to their treachery. First, though, I'd wring out all the information I could. I had to find out the names of their Russian contacts and then dispose of them.

It wasn't a simple matter of revenge for the attempts on my life. Far from it. I knew for a certainty that Martin Steel's sudden visit to the U.S. after a five-year absence had everything to do with the missile program and the inspection team coming from Russia. And the data-selling activity of the senator and his four traitor accomplices had obviously been speeded up since Steel's arrival and my discovery of his visit.

The sad part was that the senator and his friends had been selling information that they considered harmless, or reasonably so. They had no idea that each piece of data they fed to Steel's machine meant another threat on my life—and on the success of the missile program. A true case of where ignorance of the law is no excuse.

And where did Hawk fit in? Was he the dupe of men like Senator Barker and John Pesco? Had they called him after the shooting in the Holiday Inn elevator to tell him that my activities were upsetting certain sensitive areas? Was that why he'd lied and said he hadn't even known I was in St. Anthony's Hospital? Or had the senator or his friends managed to keep the truth from Hawk? No. Impossible.

Hawk was in that room. I saw him.

Okay, so I was in a safe place for now. I knew I'd never use the room again, so I might as well blow it for cover and use its phone. I called Felicia first. She was still in her apartment.

"Don't say anything," I told her. "Just start taking notes."

I told her about the senator's death and how he got that way. I told her what he'd been doing, told her to quote a "reliable government source" on the matter. I also told her that there would be four more judgment calls similar to the one on the senator, but I didn't tell her the names. For some perverse reason, I wanted Pierson, Stanton, Hutchings, and Pesco to sweat out my visits to them. They'd know that the senator talked, know that the angel of death was heading their way.

At the end of my long tale to Felicia Starr, she asked what she'd asked so many times before, what the senator had asked:

"Who are you?"

"Forest Creature," I said. "Or Woods Hunter or Cellar Dweller or Attic Fanatic. Pick a name, but refer to me as a reliable government source. Tell Jordan Alman that the man who came to visit him last night is the reliable government source."

"You went to see Jordan? What happened?"

"He'll tell you about it when you get to the office. Meanwhile, get down there and start cranking out the story I just gave you. Believe me, it's an exclusive."

I hung up and called Hawk. I knew he would be at the office waiting for my call. He was. I know him almost as well as he knows me.

"It's needless to ask," he said wearily, "but where are you?"

"Didn't N6 tell you? I got tired of the chase and took a room at the Thomas Circle Holiday . . ."

"Knock it off, N3. I've no time for jokes. I want to know what you think you're doing."

Hawk didn't know it, but I had to joke to keep it light, or I would have blown my stack at him. The mere thought that he might be a traitor—the thought of him having lied to me about being in that hospital room—made me angry. And hurt.

I told him about the senator's confession, about my killing the man. I was just starting to tell him that I'd given the story to Felicia Starr when he blew his stack.

"You damned fool! Nick, I told you to stay

away from the missile program. I told you to find Martin Steel, nothing else. I told you . . ."

"You've told me a lot of things," I said. "You . . ."

I had a feeling that the computer was about to make my location. I hung up, waited five minutes, and called again.

"Listen, Sir," I said, unable to be informal with Hawk even through my anger, "I don't want to argue with you. But the senator gave me some names of people who are traitors, who've been feeding data to the Russians. I just thank God that your name wasn't among them. I'm going after those men now."

"No!" Another bark, another sharp command, another angry blast. "You're fooling around in a very sensitive area, Nick. I just talked with the President, after you hung up, and told him what happened with the senator. He's mad as a hornet. His express orders are to pull you in, take you off the case. His very words, Nick, were this: 'Put the bastard behind bars if you have to, but keep him out of this.' Nick, if you don't come in of your own accord, I'll have to put out an arrest-order for you. Please . . ."

That cooked it. I hung up, not because I was afraid the computer would track me, but because I was sick to my stomach. Sicker than I'd been after pot-shooting the fat senator.

Treason didn't stop with Hawk. It went all the way to the Oval Office. Things were rotten all over. Very rotten.

I spent a few seconds trying to decide which order I'd disobey next. Would I go after the four men Senator Lou Barker had named, hoping they would lead me to others, or would I go directly to the missile sites to see what kind of deviltry Martin Steel and his fellow Russians might be up to there?

Instinct told me that, if I went after the four men —Pierson, Stanton, Hutchings, and Pesco—I'd wind up in a never-ending web of intrigue and treason that would keep me and Wilhelmina (not to mention Pierre and Hugo) busy for the next hundred years or so. But it would also tip the spy, Minya Stalin/Martin Steel, that I was alive, kicking, and hot on his trail.

Even if Steel was at the missile sites in Nevada or Utah, word that his chief adversary was knocking off his treacherous contacts would bring him back.

I put a check mark alongside Allen Pierson's name in my little black notebook, left Room 605 of the Holiday Inn, and went out to rent a car.

I shouldn't have been surprised when I found that Allen Pierson's house in Hampshire Knolls wasn't surrounded by guards and cops and dogs and electrified fencing. But I checked the entire area and didn't even find an old lady out walking her dog, a sure sign of a security surveillance on a "hot" target.

I shouldn't have been surprised because of what had happened during the day. Nothing had happened. I'd gone from the car rental place to my secret apartment, slept a few hours, eaten a healthy brunch and gone out to pick up a copy of the paper.

Senator Lou Barker, according to the *Times,* was found dead in his home by his butler. Cause of death, according to the coroner, was a heart attack.

Yeah. I imagine his heart did go into some kind

of attack after that hunk of lead from Wilhelmina punctured his brain.

I called the *Times* office and asked for Felicia Starr. A male voice told me she was ill today, didn't even come to the office. I called her apartment. No answer. I drove over there. The apartment was empty. I mean, *empty*. No furniture, no carpets, no pictures, no Scotch. And, of course, no Felicia.

I went to the nearest phone booth and called Hawk.

"All right," I snarled, "so you got it all covered up. But why did you have to do away with Felicia Starr? She's an innocent bystander in all this."

"Give it up, Nick," he snarled. "I don't even know what you're talking about. I do know you're to be picked up and put in chains at Fort Belvoir. Orders from the President. Please, Nick. Give it up. You're messing around in a very sensitive . . ."

I hung up. Jesus. If I heard that "sensitive" crap once more, I'd throw up again. Traitors were ripping our country apart and selling it piece by piece to the enemy and all anyone could talk about was how sensitive that missile program was, how sensitive the inspection teams were, how sensitive everything was. Well, treason is a sensitive business that requires radical surgery.

The big problem, as I saw it, didn't lie in Utah and Nevada, or with the inspection team coming from Russia, or the one preparing to head out for Russia. The problem, the sensitive area if you will, was right here in good old Washington, D.C.

A coverup was in the works. It was a master stroke of a coverup, one to make the Watergate/Nixon fiasco look like a little white lie from a kindergarten student.

The coverup not only involved the Oval Office, it involved David Hawk. It involved AXE, the most secret of all secret organizations in our nation's government.

In all my years as an AXE agent, I'd learned that David Hawk sometimes had more power and was more important than the President.

But he was either a traitor or was being led by the nose by traitors. That made him an enemy.

By taking out after the four men Senator Lou Barker had named, I'd undoubtedly come up with other names.

I hoped against hope that David Hawk's name would *not* be among them.

And so, just after midnight, I drove the rented car into the Hampshire Knolls area, expecting an army of resistance, but not really surprised when that army didn't materialize. The word had filtered down to Pierson. The man who'd killed Senator Barker had been called off. Pierson didn't have the word yet that the man wasn't taking the call.

The Pierson house was a duplicate of about two thousand houses in the Hampshire Knolls residential area. There were certain exterior variations, mostly cosmetic, but I'd hate to live there and come home with a snootful and try to find my own dolled-up abode among the clone houses that populated the area.

But I found Pierson's house with no trouble, sniffed out the area, found it clean, parked the rented car three blocks away, and went right to work. Most of the house was dark. Light glimmered through a shade at the rear and I tagged that room as the den. Pierson was working late, possibly counting his money from his Russian contacts.

I decided on the dramatic approach. Partly for surprise, partly because I wanted this kill to attract enough attention to give the coverup boys a hard time tagging it as another heart attack. I marked off a clear place in the backyard, snugged Wilhelmina in my right fist, and made a running dash for the window.

I sailed through glass and shade, did a somersault in the middle of the floor—narrowly missing a huge walnut coffee table—and came up in my killing crouch, facing a skinny, long-faced man in bathrobe and pajamas. It was Pierson. He was sitting in an armchair, early American style, with a folder on his lap. Beside the chair on the floor was an open briefcase. I pointed the Luger at Pierson's bushy left eyebrow.

"You know what I want," I growled. "You have exactly three minutes to give it to me."

I figured it would take four or five minutes for the neighbors to call the local cops and for them to get here. I was giving myself at least a minute-or-two leeway for escape.

"Who are you?" he demanded, eyeballing the Luger. He knew what was happening, knew what had happened to Senator Barker, but was stupidly stalling for time. Well, it was his time. "What do you want?"

I wasted a minute of his valuable time telling him how I'd helped the senator have his heart attack, how the senator had spilled his guts first and had named Pierson and three others as go-betweens with the Russian paymasters.

"Now," I concluded, "I want all the names you have as go-betweens, especially the name of the man who deals directly with the Soviets, and all the Russian names involved. You have a minute and fifty seconds."

He was more stupid than I had figured. I should have known. Pierson was the lowest link in the chain. If he'd had any smarts, he'd have been the senator. But he had no smarts.

He got indignant. He stood up and began to wave his arms and to shriek at me as though I'd violated his most precious rights. Which, of course, I had. And which, of course, he'd long ago forfeited by becoming a traitor.

"Whoever you are," he shrieked, "I'll have you hanged for this. The police are very protective of this area. They'll be here in seconds. No jail will be good enough for you, you son-of-a-bitch. I'll see to it . . ."

And so on . . .

I rapped off two quick shots from Wilhelmina. I hadn't put on the silencer. When those lethal whizzers boomed out of the Luger, even the wallpaper in the quiet little den seemed to shiver. Allen Pierson's mouth stopped flapping, his arms stopped waving. He checked his skinny body for wounds, but I'd put the slugs in the wall above the window I'd just violated with my flying leap.

"A minute and five seconds," I growled.

"You can't do this," he shrieked, finding his voice again. "I don't even know what you're talking about. You want money? I can give you . . ."

"I'll bet you can," I said, cutting him short. "I don't want American money that's been laundered through Moscow. You have forty-five seconds."

He chose to waste his last forty-five seconds with more protests, more shrieking, more waving of long, skinny arms. I clocked him and then pocketed Wilhelmina. I snapped Hugo into my hand and grabbed the man by the scruff of his scrawny neck. I literally threw him out the smashed window and leaped out after him.

Lights were going on in the clone houses up and down the block and across the back fence. Lights were going on upstairs in Pierson's own house. Time was awasting.

I stripped off his robe. Actually, I cut it off, in shreds, with Hugo's razor-sharp blade. I did the same with his pajamas and then led him to the back fence. I found a small wrought-iron bench and stood on it to hoist the naked, protesting, shrieking Allen Pierson to the top of the high chain-link fence. His thin buttocks and fingers clung to the bar at the top and I pulled the bench away.

In a few well-chosen words, I told Pierson that I was going to empty the remaining fourteen slugs from the Luger's clip into his skinny body and spread his guts and brains all over his neighbor's yard. He picked that moment to sing. I listened impatiently as a siren began to wail in the distance, keeping him company. Cops had been called. Cops were doing what cops were supposed to do when they were called by the prominent citizens of Hampshire Knolls. They were coming to chase out the intruder.

Pierson didn't give me any names other than those I already had from the senator. He probably didn't know any others involved, low as he was on the ladder of treason. But he admitted his own part, gave me that bullcrap about the library having the same info he'd passed along the line, and began to plead for his life.

I very nearly spared the poor sap. A well of nausea rose in my throat as I thought of what I had to do, of what I'd said I would do. Anger counteracted the nausea. Anger at Hawk and the senator. Anger at the President. Anger at the coverup of the way the senator had died. Anger at treason that was like a cancer that I could see but couldn't totally excise.

In frustration, I pressed Wilhelmina's trigger and held it down. Hot, brutal, blasting lead poured from the barrel. The quiet neighborhood came alive with the repetitive booms that seemed to meld into one long orgiastic explosion.

I watched Allen Pierson's skinny body buck and jerk on top of that fence, watched it spin backwards like a broken doll flung from a window. From behind me, I heard a woman's scream. I turned as Pierson's bloody, broken body disappeared in shrubs beyond the fence. A pretty woman in a nightgown stood on the back porch. It was obviously Pierson's wife.

She'd seen the whole thing, the brutal execution of her darling husband.

She'd never believe that her husband was a traitor, that I was anything but a brutal killer.

Extremism in the defense of liberty is no . . .

Somehow, those words were hollow in my mind. I felt like a heartless killer. I felt sick. I wanted no more of this. At that moment, I wasn't even concerned about the siren that was now quite loud. I actually wanted the police to catch me, to blow me to bits with their .38 specials.

Extremism—that is to say, total war—in the defense of liberty may not be a vice, but it is one hell of a pain in the ass.

With the image of that lovely, screaming woman in my head, I sprinted past her, past three houses, through a dark yard, over a low fence, and out onto the next street down. I circled around to my rented car just as more sirens wailed away the night's previous silence and two police cars screeched to a halt in front of Allen Pierson's house, three blocks away.

I started the car, backed up into a driveway, turned and drove six blocks before turning on the headlights.

The sickness didn't want to go away and I couldn't get up enough anger to fight it. It wasn't only sickness from what had just happened, it was sickness from what was to come during this already long night.

I had three more kills to make before dawn.

SIX

In all my years as Killmaster for AXE, I've never known a bloodier night.

Oh, I've had nights in which more people have died, but those were different. There had been shootouts in which I was hiding behind one barrier and a host of enemies behind another. The killing had an impersonal ring to it.

On that summer night in Washington, I faced each of my victims with no barriers between us. Each of my victims was unarmed, except for the guilt of treason.

Even as I told myself that such assassinations, such exterminations, were necessary because these men were traitors and because the manner of their death would make it impossible for other traitors to continue to cover up the threat to their ranks— and keep the American people in ignorance of the treason that ran amok in their capital city—the killing wasn't made any easier.

Donald Stanton came after Pierson. Stanton, as special presidential envoy to the Atomic Energy Commission, could very well have been in a vital position to feed the Soviets all they needed to know, but I doubted that he was the key link. Still, he was highly placed and had to go. He lived in an apartment (they call them townhouses now) just over three blocks from the White House.

I knew that gunfire in that location would bring out the Secret Service, the FBI, the CIA, Washington police, and all other law enforcement and/or protection agencies imbued with the noble duty of protecting human life, especially the President's. The hit on Stanton, thus, was the most dangerous for me. Perhaps that's why I decided to hit him next. A kind of death wish in action.

If they got me after I did in Stanton, I'd be saved the agony and nausea of having to do in Hutchings and Pesco.

Before I arrived at the Stanton townhouse, I stopped in an all-night drugstore and bought some things. Three large pieces of poster board. A box of crayons. A ball of twine. Sitting in the seat of the rented car, using the steering wheel as a desk, I made three signs, each with the same heading:

THIS MAN IS A TRAITOR TO HIS COUNTRY

In smaller print, I named the others, beginning with Senator Lou Barker. I signed each poster: "Forest Creature." If Felicia were still functioning, she'd know. Somehow, she'd get past the coverup boys and see that the true story was printed.

I hadn't forgotten about Felicia. It was still on my mind to pay another call on Jordan Alman, her associate editor, to find out who had shut her up, and why. Find out where she was. But the treason game took precedence.

I not only had to eliminate the traitors I knew, but to discover the names of the others. Find the link between the traitors and the missile program, or at least the inspection part of it.

There was a damned good reason why Minya Stalin/Martin Steel had shown up in Washington just two weeks before the Russian inspection team was to arrive, and before the American inspection team was to leave for Russia.

That reason had something—perhaps everything —to do with those missiles lying beneath the sandy desert soil of Nevada and Utah.

Back to Stanton.

I parked the rented car in a most obvious spot. Smack in front of Blair House, cater-cornered from the White House on Pennsylvania Avenue. I stuck a CIA card I carry, on the windshield to keep the local fuzz from towing it away and walked the three blocks to Stanton's townhouse. It was dark, as it should be at one thirty in the morning.

There was a watchman, of course. I had no quarrel with him, so I went up to him in the foyer, chatted in a friendly manner and turned to leave. As I reached the door, I dropped one of my harmless Pierres—one with nerve gas instead of lethal poison. I stood outside and watched the watchman slump behind his desk in the foyer, then lay his little head down for an hour of sleep.

I went up to Stanton's suite, kicked in the door, dragged him out of bed, sent his mistress off into the night, and gave him the same opportunity I'd given Allen Pierson. After telling him all I knew and all I'd done, I added:

"You have three minutes to tell me your part in the game, plus the names of all the others, especially the Russian contacts."

"Who are you?" he demanded.

Stanton was a big man, muscular, very-important-looking even in jockey shorts. He was accustomed to giving orders; he didn't like getting them.

Even though I disliked him immediately, I did toy with the idea of sparing his life if he told me what I wanted to know in the allotted three minutes. But he'd already messed up twenty precious seconds and I knew I'd have to scare the information out of him and then empty a clip into that handsome, muscular body.

"I'll start the three-minute timer over," I said, actually setting the timer on my Quartz wristwatch. I told him the precise details of my dealings with Allen Pierson, told him I'd probably let him live if he used his three minutes properly. "Okay," I said, "the three minutes start now."

"Who are you? What do you mean barging in here waving that stupid pistol around? How did you get past the watchman? Don't you know who I am? Don't you know I can have you . . ."

And so on.

Talk about slow learners.

I squeezed off a shot and took away about a third of his left ear. The slug went on past, carrying flesh, gristle, skin and blood all the way to the wall of the expensively-decorated living room. Stanton was standing beside a highboy desk; he'd passed up my invitation to relax in one of his comfortable Sheraton chairs.

The roar of Wilhelmina and the scream of Stanton merged in the room, but not much sound reached the street. I went over, knocked out a front window, came back and squeezed off another missile of pain.

The slug took away a third of his right ear.

This time, the sounds of gunfire and human screaming streaked into the quiet of Fifteenth Street. Hopefully, all the way to the Secret Service quarters at the White House.

"Two minutes, eighteen seconds," I said. "I'll extend the time if you start saying the things I want to hear. It's up to you, you treacherous bastard."

He had both hands to his ears, like someone trying to shut out things he didn't want to hear. Blood was seeping through his thick fingers. The real show was in his eyes, though. He had large brown eyes, very intelligent looking. His eyebrows were even and well trimmed. He had an almost regal look about him, as though royalty lurked somewhere in his heritage. It was a pity he was such an overbearing ass. And a traitor to boot. But then, perhaps those traits are common to royalty. Who am I to say?

I suddenly realized that I couldn't give this man his whole three minutes. That last shot and scream would bring a swift response here in the heart of the capital. The Secret Service is just a tad quicker than suburban cops.

I squeezed the trigger and an arrow of flame and sound erupted from Wilhelmina's barrel. The bullet went right where I aimed it. It took away three knuckles of his left hand, the one that had been holding his damaged left ear. Without hesitation, I ripped off another shot and removed four knuckles of his right hand.

All the royal pomp went out of him then. He screeched and howled and danced around the room like something demented and beset by monsters. He swore, he cried, he bellowed. And all that horrible sound leaked out the window into the Washington night.

"Talk!" I shouted above his shouting. "Goddamn you, talk."

I was sweating from tension and nausea. Sweat made the Luger go slack in my hand. A kind of fear made my body tremble. It wasn't fear of being caught here by the police or the Secret Service. As I said before, I almost welcomed that. It was fear of what I was doing, fear that I was becoming even more of a monster than the man dancing and howling around the room.

I was about to dash from the room, away from the terror and agony that I was inflicting on my victim, when he began to talk. He kept on dancing around the room and howling every now and then, but he kept up a fairly steady stream of information.

His Russian contact, he said, was a man named Natoly Dobrinka, a member of the Russian Embassy staff. His American go-between, the man he fed information to give to Dobrinka, was Harold Brookman, a chief aide to the secretary of defense.

My sweating grew instead of diminishing. Harold Brookman was a far more important man that his title signified. As a confidant to the secretary of defense, he had access to information so secret that not even the President was briefed on much of it. But his information was always contingent on what other departments were doing. Brookman was obviously the key member of this gang of traitors. He needed others to fill in and make his own information of value to the enemy.

"Is Brookman the key man?" I demanded. "Is

he the key man, or is there someone higher than him?"

"I don't know," Stanton shrieked. "For the love of God, who are you?"

I didn't answer. I had all I was going to get from this man, and the night was filling up with sirens. My next shot was an act of mercy. The man had to have been in excruciating pain.

He stood for a full five seconds after Wilhelmina's husky slug blew out the back of his skull. Then, he sagged to the floor, out of pain, out of misery, out of royalty, out of the treason game. I draped the sign around his neck. It rested across his flat, athletic stomach. What a waste, I thought: all that good food, exercise, and money down the drain for an inveterate coward and traitor.

It was no good going downstairs. Fifteenth Street was full of unmarked cars. The sirens were getting louder, indicating the imminent arrival of the black and whites of the Washington police.

I went up the staircase to the roof, leaped from roof to roof, and came to a fire escape on the K Street side of the building. I went down, ran all the way to Seventeenth, cut south to the Mall, then back to the rented car in front of Blair House. I pocketed the CIA card, got in, let the trembling run its course and drove away from there. I headed out on Pennsylvania Avenue toward Georgetown —and the home of Leland Hutchings.

Hutchings, the administrative assistant to the chairman of the Senate's Nuclear Energy Committee, lived in a two-hundred-year-old cottage on Thirty-Seventh Street, just off S Street in northwest

Georgetown. Quiet street in a quiet section of a quiet D. C. district. Georgetown is an entity of its own, separated from downtown Washington by Rock Creek Gorge, and as old as the country itself. Benjamin Franklin lived there when he wasn't trying to screw all the young ladies of Paris. The Exorcist did his work in Georgetown.

Tonight, an exorcist of another stripe had come to Georgetown.

The kill was made easy by the fact that Leland Hutchings was a far greater ass than was Donald Stanton. He apparently hadn't believed the word that the killer of Senator Barker had been called off. He was waiting in his dark living room with a shotgun. Twelve gauge. Big enough to blow away a third of my body, much less one of my ears.

But the dumb ass couldn't lay off the cigarettes long enough to make his vigil work. I saw the red glow through the curtains as he sucked smoke into his nervous lungs. I'd parked the car up on T Street and had circled the block three times before I saw the glow of Hutching's cigarette.

My first thought was to toss one of the nerve-gas Pierres through the window and put him to sleep. But I didn't have an hour to waste. There was John Pesco to go. And, if dawn didn't overtake me, there were Harold Brookman and Natoly Dobrinka. And, of course, whatever names Hutchings might provide me. The night could be longer and bloodier than I'd anticipated.

I chose my second thought, a repeat of my surprise entry into the home of Allen Pierson.

I dove through a rear window, heard the thunderous blast of the twelve-gauge shotgun as every nerve in Hutching's body must have let loose at the same time. I came to my feet against a back wall of the living room in which Leland Hutchings sat shooting off his weapon. He apparently heard me hit the wall and came to his senses enough to cut loose with another round.

Buckshot accompanied the deafening roar. It rumbled through the plaster and whistled through the bedroom into which I'd propelled myself. I didn't even consider that he might be using a double-barrelled gun. There are so many automatics that you can't figure such things anymore.

Although Hutchings did have a double-barrelled job, he didn't have any extra shells. I had inadvertently suckered him into blowing his whole wad. And he hadn't the good sense to let me wonder about it. He dashed into the bedroom swinging the damned shotgun by the barrel.

I moved to a corner and let him wear himself down a bit. He hit walls, windows, bureaus, the bed, pictures, a mirror and just about everything in the room but me. He was a wild man without a sense of purpose or direction. His long wait for me must have been driving him crazy, and now it was all coming out.

"I'll kill you, you sonofabitching bastard cocksucker, you," he screamed as he pulverized a portrait of some long-ago relative. "You won't get anything out of me. I've got your number, you fucking Mafia-loving government executioner. If you had any sense, you'd know that the only way is through communism and . . ."

And so on.

All the while he was spouting the Party line, he was swinging that silly shotgun. The walnut stock was turning to splinters, but he was still doing a pretty fair job of demolishing the room. I was starting to be afraid that he'd accidentally hit a piece of glass and send it flying my way. I knew his type. He was a hard-liner, a true believer in the bullshit that pours out of Moscow. He wouldn't talk if I shot off *six* ears.

So, I caught him in mid-swing. The roar of Wilhelmina stopped him even before the bullet crashed into his brain. He let the shotgun fall and just stood there staring at me with unbelieving eyes.

"Say hello to old Joe," I said as he tumbled to the floor. I meant Joe Stalin, of course, but he wasn't hearing me.

I had the sign draped around his neck and was out of there long before the sirens rent the quiet night air. To make sure the cops didn't forget where the action was, I squeezed off four clear, well-spaced shots into Leland Hutching's front yard before I walked up to T Street and my trusty rented car.

At precisely two thirty in the morning, I stopped half a mile north of the home of John Pesco. He had a fancy mansion up along Rock Creek Gorge, a few miles past the National Zoological Gardens, in Barnaby Woods. His title and his house fit each other as snugly as a surgeon's rubber gloves.

As White House chief of staff, John Pesco had been one of the most popular men in America. He had virtually taken over the duties of the President's press secretary. His name and face became as familiar to American television audiences as Johnny Carson. It was his popularity and ambition, however, that had forced the President to make him chief deputy to Charles Ajax. It got him out of the limelight and the President back in it.

It also got him into a choice spot for the Russians to lay down some laundered American money.

My anger, that had lain in the background during the unsavory disposal of Allen Pierson and Donald Stanton, was running at full throttle now. Leland Hutchings had fueled it, reminded me of what the war was all about.

These men, I was convinced, were far worse than enemy soldiers across an empty field or hunkered in behind sandbags. They were cancerous traitors posing as patriots. With an enemy soldier, you knew where you stood. You shot at him and he shot at you, all because the politicians of your nation had decided that was what you were supposed to do.

The enemy soldier was just as innocent and pure in his profession as you were in yours.

This wasn't so with men like John Pesco. These men had raped the nation, had endeared themselves to their own people and busied themselves with selling those people out.

I looked forward to the killing of John Pesco.

But other forces were at work. Forces that I had expected earlier, forces that hadn't materialized, forces that, by their absence, had lulled me into a sense of safety.

As I stepped from the rented car, after cruising past John Pesco's mansion on Jones Road for a quick inspection, I heard the distinctive crack of a high-velocity, ultra-powered rifle. It came from quite some distance, but I'd heard that sound before. Many times.

It was the sound of a Russian AK47.

A split second before the copper-sheathed bullet reached me, and a full second before the AK47 began to chatter like a vicious magpie, I hit the dirt beside the car.

The first slug took out the window of the door I had just opened. The volley of slugs virtually decimated the car from hood to taillights.

The next volley, I knew, would be lower, down where I was lying on my belly.

SEVEN

It takes but three seconds to change the clip on an AK47. I knew that my would-be killer was in a hurry, so he'd chop a fraction of a second off that time. If the killer were Martin Steel, he'd chop off a whole second.

In two seconds flat, I rolled from the side of the car to the edge of the short cliff that runs along the western edge of Jones Mill Road. I was dropping the few feet to a grassy ledge when the AK47 cut loose again.

Dirt above me kicked loose as the lethal missiles hurled themselves pell mell into the bank. Dirt showered down on me. The air was filled with the tak-tak-tak-tak-tak sound of the murderous Russian weapon. I estimated the gunman's distance from me at a half mile, but not the half mile to John Pesco's mansion. Those bullets were coming from somewhere down in the gorge.

Either by instinct or by foolhardiness, I was fleeing for safety right into the teeth of my merchant of death. Instinct told me I had to eliminate the threat to my life. Foolhardiness told me that I could best do it by exposing my life to greater danger.

In the next hiatus of just above two seconds, while another clip was being jammed into place, I rolled down a grassy slope, landed behind a thick walnut tree, and hustled Wilhelmina into my hand. The next salvo tried its best to rip the tree trunk from in front of me, but the walnut wood held its own pretty well. I used the next respite to dash farther down the slope, into the murky darkness of Rock Creek Park. There were trees galore, but each time I hid behind one, the gunman found the spot and hurled another clipload of copper and lead into it. At the rate we were going, we would have the whole park shredded into toothpicks long before dawn.

In one long respite, I made it all the way to Rock Creek, crouched behind a boulder and listened to the tak-tak-tak-tak-tak sound again. Next came the hammering of slugs against the other side of the boulder. Chips of stone flew high in the air and showered me good. I held my ground and took a few quick peeks around one side.

I saw the flames from the muzzle high among the treetops, not more than two hundred yards directly west. I ducked back as the sound came, followed closely by the hammering of copper and lead on stone.

I had a very healthy respect for the AK47. The Kalashnikov assault rifle blew out 7.62mm cupro-steel slugs at high velocity and at rapid speed. It was especially accurate over long distances, could be fired singly, semi-automatic, or fully automatic. Used to the max, the Kalashnikov AK47 could eliminate a platoon of soldiers in just under ten seconds. And Minya Stalin was probably using a sniperscope, an infrared devil of a device that enabled the spy to count every whisker on my face from three hundred yards away, in pitch dark!

I decided to let him empty one more clip before dashing closer, toward another boulder or tree. I waited, hand clenching the Luger, heart pounding like the gunman's bullets. Nothing. He was trying to sucker me out of my safe spot. I started counting.

When I got to a hundred, I snaked Wilhelmina around the side of the boulder and laced the treetop with eight quick rounds, then pulled my hand back for the return fire of the AK47.

There was no return fire. I knew I hadn't hit him, even though I'd fired at the spot where I'd seen the tongues of flame from the automatic rifle. Then why was there no return fire?

I took a few counts to try and figure out the answer to that question. There was no return fire because there was no one there anymore to return the fire. Next question: Where was he?

And then it came. Christ, the guy really had suckered me. He knew my habits, my instincts. He knew I'd come after him if I survived that first shot, that first volley. Now that he had me in the gorge, he would spring his trap.

All right. What was his trap? To circle around behind me and get me from the side of the boulder on which I was hiding? Possibly. Did he have allies waiting to move in on me while I was trying to figure out why he'd stopped firing? No. I knew enough about Minya Stalin to know that he always worked this kind of gig alone.

So, he was obviously circling to come up behind me, between me and Jones Mill Road, between me and the mansion of one John Pesco. Okay, I'd play his game.

I backed away from the boulder, surveyed the slopes and woods I'd just come through, saw and heard nothing, then took off at a dead run toward the south, toward the zoo. I knew Stalin's circling technique. He always came around to his right, never his left. His right would be north, so I would circle south and catch him on the fly.

I guessed right. He circled north, but he didn't come on down into my trap. I was holed up three hundred yards down the creek and saw a shadow move in close to the boulder where I'd been hiding. The shadow disappeared and I didn't see it again.

What now?

He was waiting for me to lose patience and come looking for him. He'd deliberately crossed an area with backlight, in an upright position, to give me a good gander at his shadow, or his silhouette. Then he'd lie low and wait me out. That was his bait and I was the fish that was supposed to take it.

Well, fishing season was over for this night. I wouldn't tumble, I wouldn't play. I slipped out of the little grass-covered nook where I'd been hiding beside the trickling creek and made my way from tree to tree, boulder to boulder, heading south toward the zoo. At the Military Road Bridge, I climbed up to the street and hailed a taxi coming from the direction of Chevy Chase, the section of Washington where so many of the wealthy live.

For the cabbie, stopping was a big mistake. I had figured Martin Steel/Minya Stalin all wrong. He had figured me right.

I had just opened the door of the cab when the night exploded with tak-tak-tak-tak-tak sounds. I hit the pavement, but the cabbie had no idea what the hell was going on. What came down was a volley of copper-sheathed slugs that killed him and made a junker of his new Dodge taxi.

In the three-second interval while Steel was jamming in a new curved clip, I sprinted down toward Missouri Avenue. I had cut between houses, leaped fences, fought off dogs, ducked clotheslines and crossed street after street before I realized I had lost all sense of direction. I ran until my side was splitting, until the bullet wound was gushing blood instead of seeping it.

And I kept on running.

As lethal as Wilhelmina is, she's no match for an AK47. What my Luger can hit at fifty yards, an AK47 in the hands of Martin Steel can hit at several times that distance. There would be another day, another time, another bloody night.

If I lived through this one.

I lived through it, but just barely. I ran all the way to McMillan Reservoir, a distance of almost forty blocks, before every piece of my mechanism gave out. I found a concrete pump house, crawled in, and lay panting with exhaustion. I had just enough energy to hold my Luger in one hand and my stiletto in the other. I watched the open door of the little concrete shed, waiting for Martin Steel and his magic AK47.

He didn't show. Either his energy gave out or he was sitting back at John Pesco's mansion chortling over a cup of tea. Or vodka. I fell asleep. At dawn I awoke and felt worse. I tore a piece of material from my shirt and jammed it beneath the bandage to stop the flow of blood. My slacks and loafers were soaked in the red stuff.

It was a classic case of the hunter becoming the hunted. The victor becoming the victim. I was tempted to roust myself from the pump house and go scouting for a nice compact M16 automatic rifle to counter the AK47, but I've never had much use for those long-distance murder devices. I like close work, detail work. I like to see the results of my skills.

On the other hand, it seemed foolish to go on literally fighting tanks with pitchforks, as the Hungarians did in 1956. I couldn't go against Martin Steel with my puny weapons, not when he seemed to have my moves laid out on his brain like a blueprint.

A thought came. Perhaps the gunman wasn't Steel at all. Perhaps it was N6, or another AXE agent, sent by Hawk to button me up for good. No. Hawk wouldn't do that.

Another thought came. I'd killed Senator Lou Barker, then had gone after the four men he'd named as his associates. I'd had no trouble until I got to John Pesco.

What made John Pesco so damned important that Martin Steel (or any gunman) would be there to protect him?

He was the first deputy to Charles Ajax, the man who headed the missile program. That made him perhaps the most important link of all to the Russians, especially in view of the impending inspections by both nations of the others' newest nuclear capabilities.

All the others, the senator included, were just so much featherbedding, excess baggage.

All this cerebral activity led me to a new potential. I wondered if Charles Ajax knew that his chief deputy was on the Soviet payroll, lived in a fancy mansion that had to cost a couple of million laundered dollars, and was protected by Russia's most exclusive and successful spy and executioner.

And I wondered where Martin Steel had been all this time since his attempt to blow me apart in that Holiday Inn elevator. In Utah or Nevada at the missile site? Possibly. If so, what had he been doing there? Would he return to finish whatever he'd been doing once he'd disposed of me and made his chief contact—John Pesco—safe again?

As usual, my cerebral activity conjured up more questions than answers. I needed a good long talk with David Hawk. If he had turned his coat around and was one of them, at least he could give me an indication of just what I was facing. You sometimes learn more jawing with an enemy than an ally anyway.

All right. As much as I disliked the idea, I'd get out of that cold, clammy pump house and do the phone-booth-hopping trick.

The day came up unusually sunny and I looked a sight walking down North Capitol Street from the reservoir. I hailed six cabs, but none stopped. I found a drugstore at the Randolph Street intersection, across the street from McKinley High School. The place was full of teenagers and they giggled at my bloody trousers and loafers. They were either a ghoulish bunch of teens or they thought I was in some kind of costume. You never know with today's teens.

Hawk was still at home, as I expected him to be. Good, I wouldn't have to worry about the computer until he'd rung in on his other phone and put the technicians at headquarters to work.

I brought him up to date on things, then posed a few questions:

"What have they done with Felicia Starr? What does our intelligence network have to say about Martin Steel and the missile sites as they pertain to the upcoming visit by the Soviet inspection team? Is Charles Ajax clean or dirty? Why did the newspapers leave out the real reason for Senator Lou Barker's death? What's your part in this filthy business and why can't you level with me?"

And so on.

Hawk listened with growing impatience. It was reflected through his occasional grunts, and the grinding of his teeth. When I'd finished with my questions, he said:

"Nick, I can only tell you one thing. The President himself has ordered you to be picked up and put in jail until this inspection business is over. If you resist, you're to be killed. When everything settles down, he'll discuss what to do about the murders you've . . ."

"Murders!" I exploded. "Jesus Christ, if I'd killed men with half the guilt of these traitorous bastards, I'd get a medal. Why is everything so different now?"

"I can only tell you one . . ."

"Oh, can it!" I said, then added, "Sir."

I hung up. His lips obviously were sealed, either by the President or by his Russian owners. I preferred to think the former. Treachery just didn't seem to fit David Hawk. And yet . . .

I put aside such thoughts and called Jordan Alman at home. I would have preferred another personal visit, but time was awasting again. I had two questions for him.

"Where's Felicia Starr? Why haven't you printed the truth about Senator Lou Barker?"

"Felicia hasn't shown up for work since the day after you broke in and threatened me with a gun," he said calmly and with a modicum of indignation. He was still smarting over that gun barrel being pressed into his forehead until it made a red ring. "I don't know where she is. As for Senator Barker, we printed the truth as we knew it. You know, young man, we don't make the news. We depend on certain reliable sources . . ."

"Oh, cut it."

I hung up and called the home of Charles Ajax. A servant with a thick European accent answered and said Mr. Ajax was out of town. Mrs. Ajax? She was asleep. Would I leave a message? I hung up and sat on a stool between two teenagers to get some breakfast into my guts.

Through eggs, bacon, and homefries, I let my mind roam again. I was getting nowhere now, and getting there faster than ever. I was tired, weak from loss of blood, in pain, and wounded in dignity from my middle-of-the-night flight from an AK47 and the madman who used it so skillfully.

To make matters worse, my mind refused to roam in the proper directions. Like a computer nearing burnout, it had literally shut itself off. I could barely function as a human machine, much less as an adversary for a man like Martin Steel.

I finished breakfast, barged into a cab when the driver stopped at a red light, gave him an address six blocks from my secret apartment, got mean when he insisted that he had another call to make, and relaxed in the seat. I relaxed so much that the driver had to wake me when we got to the destination.

Wearily, I stumbled along in the wrong direction, just in case the cabdriver would be questioned (or, in my paranoia, in case he was an enemy agent), circled a block, and finally made it to my apartment. I slept like the dead, only barely grateful that I was alive. I dreamed that I was in a phone booth and the phone kept ringing and ringing and ringing.

About four P.M., I awoke, bolted down a quick meal of Wheaties, powdered milk, and half-frozen bread, then went out for a newspaper. I still had on the bloody clothes. The fact is, I just didn't care anymore, I was that worn out.

When I was safely back in the apartment, I unfolded the newspaper and ran through it from the front page to the comics. There was nothing more about Senator Barker. And nothing on the front page about Allen Pierson, Donald Stanton, and Leland Hutchings. Inside, there were three separate obits on the government officials. I wasn't overjoyed to learn that officially they'd all died of heart attacks. In their sleep.

A small item at the bottom of the obit page caught my eye, but only for a second. It was about an unidentified but well-dressed man whose body had been fished from the Potomac across from the Lincoln Memorial. The spot was just downriver from the Theodore Roosevelt Memorial Bridge, a favorite jumping-off spot for drug addicts, drunks, and other screwed-up crazies.

I let it pass, fuming over the casual and untrue treatment of the three kills I'd spent so much time trying to make elaborate enough to hit the news in a big way. Somebody high up was really making it a fulltime job to cover my bloody tracks.

I was still fuming, and considering paying anoth-

r call on Jordan Alman, the dignified associate editor of the Washington *Times*, when the phone rang. I damned near leaped out of my skin.

Years ago, when I'd taken this apartment under another name, I'd had a phone put in. I'd paid extra for an unlisted number. The damned thing had never rung, and I'd used it only to call up a date or to send out for pizza. I'd never called Hawk or AXE headquarters on it. There was no way anyone could have traced that phone to me.

But it was ringing.

Ah, I thought, a wrong number. I would just let it ring and the caller would soon give up. But the phone kept ringing. The sound was driving me nuts. It finally stopped. I went into the bedroom and shucked the bloody clothes and hopped into the shower. The bullet wound looked wicked, so I put on a new bandage and took a couple of sulfa tablets when I got out of the shower. I was dressing in slacks and putting on shoes when the phone started to ring again. Jesus, maybe I hadn't been dreaming earlier.

On the fifteenth ring, I picked up the receiver. I didn't say anything, just stuck the damned thing to my ear.

"Woods Hunter?"

It was Felicia Starr. My God, the fake name I'd used to rent the apartment and put in the phone was the same fake name I'd given her the first time she asked who I was. I almost yodeled with joy, then felt a tightening of my security glands. Watch it. People can imitate voices, just as they can disguise themselves as others.

"Woods, I know you're there. I can hear you breathing. Would you rather I call you Forest Creature?"

It was definitely Felicia.

"Where are you?" I said. "How did you get this number? What's going on? Where have you been? Who . . ."

"Hold on, Mister Secret," she said, using another phony but apropos name. "One thing at a time. I've been looking all over for you. Don't forget, I'm a newspaperwoman. I have my sources. The important thing is that you and I are both still alive. We have a great deal to talk about. I want to come up."

"You know where I live?"

"I do. I would have come instead of calling, but I was afraid you'd shoot and ask questions later. I'm just down the block, in a drugstore."

What would the world do without drugstores?

She was the loveliest sight I'd seen in days. Although anything would have looked good after all those fat and skinny bodies being blown apart by Wilhelmina's nasty bite, Felicia Starr was perhaps the best visual medicine I could have found. And I didn't find her; she found me.

"Nice place," she said, breezing in with her auburn hair flying, her deep blue eyes sparkling, her freckles glistening, her ample breasts bouncing. "Much better than where I've been holed up."

She turned at my portable bar and I must have looked like a kid watching Santa Clause come down the chimney. She held out her arms and the last vestiges of all my suspicion went swirling down the drain like little cleaning bubbles.

Soft moments followed.

Felicia clucked over my wound when we were naked and on my bed. She kissed the red, swollen area around it, put on a fresh bandage, moved up along my body to kiss my swollen lips (somewhere in Rock Creek Gorge I'd cracked my mouth against a tree) and darted her tongue into my ears.

We both purred like kittens as we explored each other's bodies. She was as good in bed as her full body and wide smile promised to be. I stroked those ample breasts and found the distended nipples with my lips and tongue. I kissed all the parts, from her freckled forehead to her painted toenails, lingering with great relish at the auburn mound between her long, slender, but very strong legs.

Before long, our sounds weren't so soft anymore. Passion made our movements and our language more urgent, less languid. She spread those long, slender, but very strong legs and I entered her with a hardness that I didn't think myself capable of accomplishing. She wrapped those legs around my back, careful not to put pressure on the bandage over my wound.

"Whoever you are," she whispered as we began a slow, heat-building motion that threatened to drive us both crazy, "you're one hell of a lover."

Flattery got her every last ounce of my energy. When we had both climaxed, simultaneously, there wasn't anything left, and we fell into peaceful sleep.

When we woke up, the necessary talk began.

I didn't like at all what had been happening to her since I'd involved her in this mess. Or, to put it more correctly, since she'd involved herself by taking a flying leap at the man who would have been my executioner.

EIGHT

"They came not ten minutes after you called to tell me what you'd done with Senator Lou Barker," Felicia told me as we lay on the bed. "I don't know who they were, but they looked like Secret Service types. You know, clean cut, clean shaven, dull suits all the same kind."

"They weren't Secret Service," I said hotly, defensively. "They wouldn't let themselves become involved in kidnapping a woman, no matter what the reason."

She arched an eyebrow and went on, carefully avoiding casting new aspersions on the Secret Service.

"Whoever they were," she said, "there were six of them. They moved everything out of my apartment and put it in a big truck. I was shoved in with the furniture and two men got in with me. I sat in the dark, on my own couch, as the truck rambled all over hell and creation. After about ten hours, the truck stopped and one of the men got out. I saw trees and a lake, then the door was closed again. I didn't know where we were. I still don't."

"Didn't they talk? Didn't they tell you why they were hustling you and your furniture around like that?"

"They were silent as tombs. I even put a move on the man guarding me on the couch, but he didn't respond. Ice. All of them, pure ice. I asked them to let me call my boss, to tell Jordan Alman that I wasn't deliberately cutting work. They didn't answer. I played on every human sympathy I could think of, but nothing worked. The ice men just looked at me and kept their silence. Jesus, they were like monks who'd taken some kind of holy oath."

"And you've been in the back of that truck ever since the day after the senator got his?"

She shuddered.

"No. The truck moved around for the first day, then stopped. The ice men let me go to the bathroom. It was night. They took me into some trees and watched while I squatted on the ground like some damned dog. You'd think our government would at least provide its victims some toilet paper and . . ."

"It wasn't our government," I said, still on the defensive about that. "Look, I can't tell you everything, but the Russians are deep in this thing. There are some people in the government going along, but you can't blame the whole government for a few bad apples."

She threw me a curious look. "You work for the government, don't you? As defensive as you are, I'd say it was the Secret Service. Tell me, is that true?"

"Something like it," I said. "Go on with your story."

"Not much else to tell. The next day they took

me to a cabin in some deep woods and drove the
truck away. The cabin was filthy and full of
spiders. I even found an empty snakeskin on the
windowsill of the little bedroom where they put
me. I didn't sleep a wink in that place. I was waiting for that damned snake to come back and crawl
back into his skin—or into mine." She shuddered
again. "God, it was creepy."

"And the men never spoke a word?"

"Not to me, but I heard them talking in the living room from time to time. I heard names mentioned, but I don't know in what context. I heard a
name like Dobrynin."

"Dobrynin is a Russian bigwig. You sure it
wasn't Dobrinka?"

"That's it. Natoly Dobrinka. And there was a
John Pesco mentioned. They talked a lot about
Senator Barker and someone named Brooklyn."

"Brookman?"

"I guess so." She pursed her lips, then bright-
ened. "My God, you don't mean Harold
Brookman, the chief aide to the secretary of defense?"

"The same. Go on. Any other names?"

"None that I remember. Are you going to tell me
what's going on?"

"Later," I said. "Tell me how you got away from
them."

"It was yesterday morning, just before dawn.
They'd all been drinking heavily and I knew they'd
be strung out and hung over. I worked on that window, the one with the snakeskin on the sill, and got
it loose. I climbed through and ran through the
woods. I hadn't gone a hundred yards when I saw
a light go on in the cabin and heard them shouting.
They—my God, you're right—they weren't U. S.

government agents. I'd forgotten about that shouting until now. They'd spoken excellent English all the time I'd been listening in that bedroom. But the morning I took off, they were shouting in a foreign language."

"Russian?"

"I don't know. It sounded like a tape recorder being run backwards at normal speed."

"It was Russian," I said. "Go on."

"Not much more to tell. They kept shouting. They went off in several different directions and I ran like the wind."

Felicia had been in Virginia, across from Palisades Park and across the Potomac. She'd made her way to the river, talked a fisherman into bringing her to the Washington side of the river, had found a taxi and had gone to the Union Hotel two blocks from the White House. From there she'd contacted a few trusted friends, and then tried to find me. None of them knew anyone by the names of Woods Hunter or Forest Creature. She finally decided to check out a friend with the telephone company, using all the crazy names I'd given her. She'd gotten my number yesterday afternoon and had been calling ever since. I *had* heard the phone ringing while I was taking my nap. It hadn't been a dream.

"I didn't trust anyone," she said, turning and looking at me with frightened, little-girl eyes. "I wanted to call Jordan Alman at the newspaper, but I didn't know if he was in on the deal or not. When I found out that the senator's death was listed as a heart attack, I became suspicious of everyone. I knew that the only man I could trust was you. And I didn't know your damned name."

"Sorry about that. It won't help to know now, but my name is Nick Carter. I work for the government, as you suspected. Beyond that, I can't tell you anything. Except what I've learned while you and your furniture were rolling around in a truck."

I told her about the kills, about the new names I'd been given, about my suspicions of my own boss, about my harrowing night in Rock Creek Gorge.

"Obviously," I added, "there's a whole team of Russians working in the area. Your phone must have been tapped and that's why they nabbed you, to keep you from repeating what I'd told you about the senator. There's a very large conspiracy of treason afoot in this country and it all has to do with the Russian inspection team coming to visit our missile site. Martin Steel, the man who was about to finish me off in that elevator when you hit him with a flying tackle, is the advance man for whatever plans the Russians have in mind. He's also the top Soviet spy, a vicious killer who will come after you when this is over."

"Why would he come after me?"

"Revenge. You stopped him from killing me. He'll move heaven and earth to get revenge, no matter how innocent you might be."

As soon as the shock had run its course through her mind, her face softened. She smiled and traced a finger down my chest to my pubic region. There was a rustling of activity down there.

"I'm hardly innocent," she said with a low, sultry voice, "thanks to you." And once more we took a moment to lose ourselves in one another. But this time our lovemaking was less frantic and more gentle. And afterwards we fell into a long, much-needed sleep. We didn't awaken until the next morning.

After a breakfast of Wheaties, powdered milk, and toast, we sat on my couch to discuss strategy. She had a couple of newspaper friends she could trust. I had a few buddies in the Secret Service I could trust. We set about calling them.

It had been my intention to get a team of trusted patriots, people in the know whose loyalty to America was unquestionable, and get to the bottom of the conspiracy. I needed to find out just how deep—or how high—the corruption went. It was no good going after the extreme cases like Allen Pierson, Donald Stanton, and Leland Hutchings. We had to find the top traitor and work down from there.

"It's no use," she said after she'd called six people who worked for the *Times,* and one who was a senatorial aide on the Hill. "Someone really big has them all pretty scared. I'm lucky they even admitted knowing me."

I tried my buddies, four of them. Same results. The word was out. Nick Carter was a criminal, a murderer, even though no official source would even admit publicly that any murders had been committed. Not a line in any newspaper, not a word on any radio or television news program.

There was one thing—one word—in common with all of the sources Felicia and I called.

Sensitive.

The whole nature of the problem was so very, very sensitive that the topic was forbidden, even in discussion.

"Sorry, Nick, but I don't even remember that you called and asked me about this. Give it up before you mess up a really sensitive . . ."

I hung up on each of my Secret Service buddies and didn't dare try anyone else. The handwriting was all over every official wall in Washington. We don't discuss the missile program as it pertains to the coming Russian inspection team. We especially don't discuss it with Nick Carter.

Felicia finally called Jordan Alman to ask him why he hadn't printed the truth about the senator's death, or about the deaths of Allen Pierson, Donald Stanton, and Leland Hutchings.

"No comment, Felicia," he said dryly. I knew he'd said it because I was on the extention listening. "Where have you been?"

"Listen, you creampuff," Felicia snarled, losing her cool, "if you've been brainwashed into refusing to see the truth, how the hell can I expect you to believe what's been happening with me? How do I know you weren't in on it?"

"Felicia, listen. You're dealing in a really sensitive . . ."

"Oh, shut up," she said.

She hung up. She was learning fast.

I tried one more longshot and called the office of Charles Ajax, the man who was nominally the head of the missile program. He had to know about his chief deputy, John Pesco, had to know that the man was not only a traitor, but was so important to the Russians that they'd put a crack killer out to protect him.

"I'm sorry," an aide said, "but Mr. Ajax is out of town."

"Is he in Utah? Nevada?"

"I'm sorry, but Mr. Ajax is out of town. May I take a message?"

"No," I said and hung up.

I made up my mind what I would do. If the killer was lurking around John Pesco's house, I'd let him wait in vain. There was time to take care of him and Pesco later. I had to sit down eyeball to eyeball with Charles Ajax. I had to know if he knew what I knew. If he didn't know, I had to set him straight. That team of Russians would be here in a few days.

Felicia didn't like it, but I refused categorically to take her west with me.

"I'm a free agent and a citizen," she said hotly. "I can go anywhere I damned please. Besides, I'm a newspaperwoman and I want to be where the story develops."

"I can appreciate all that," I said, patient with her because I really liked the lady. "I won't throw any of that 'sensitive' bullcrap at you, but I will tell you this. If I'm to get through to Charles Ajax that his program is in danger, I won't be able to do it with a reporter along. And I figured the grapevine will work fast and Martin Steel will be at the missile site about a half-step behind me. I don't want you in his very accurate gunsights."

"I'm a big girl," she said. "I can survive any risks you can survive."

"That's the point," I said. "If Steel shows up before I get to Ajax, I probably won't survive." My memory of that night in the gorge when that AK47 was working over the trees and boulders made me shudder.

She hugged me then, thinking of what I'd said. "I want you to survive," she said softly. "We still have a lot of unfinished business together."

"I know. But my chances of making it there and back alive are far better if I go alone."

"You're right. I'll stay low until you get back."

"Where will you be? At the Union Hotel?"

She smiled impishly and her freckles turned a deep brown. "I'll be right here. I hope you don't mind if I get something in here besides Wheaties, powdered milk, and frozen bread."

"Be my guest."

When I left her, a part of me stayed behind. There was something special about Felicia Starr. She was not only beautiful, but intelligent. She also had guts. The combination was hard to resist.

I left the apartment with the terrible foreboding that I'd never see her alive again.

For once, I hoped that my gut feeling proved wrong.

NINE

The little commuter plane out of Las Vegas circled Pilot Peak at the northern end of the Pequop Mountain Range just west of the great Salt Lake Desert and the Utah border. I was already weary from the long flight to Denver, a two-hour layover, and the shorter hop into Las Vegas. After an hour there, losing money in the slot machines just outside the security checkpoint, I'd boarded the small turboprop for the trip to the northern regions of Nevada and Utah.

The plane circled Pilot Peak a second time and dropped down through rippling airdrafts to the town of Wendover, Utah. I call it a town; most people would call it a small smudge on a vast desert of white salt and sand.

The headquarters for the missile program was inside the Wendover Proving Grounds, forty miles southwest. Access by the public was forbidden. The missile tunnels themselves snaked out from the proving grounds, crossed the border and stretched almost as far as U.S. 93, that ran up through eastern Nevada from the Mexican to the Canadian borders.

Before trying to reach Charles Ajax at the headquarters site, I wanted to check some of the other sectors where the Russian inspection team would visit. I rented a car at the tiny airport and drove back across the border into Nevada, then headed south toward the Goshute Indian Reservation. The Indians there had been the most violent and vociferous opponents to the missile program, although ranchers in the area had been almost as fiercely against it.

The area residents had good arguments. Not only did the vast network of tunnels upset the ecology and make much of the land worthless for grazing cattle, but the existence of the missiles on their never-ending journeys through the tunnels made the area a prime target in a nuclear war that all were convinced would come—and come soon.

Well, that was something for the politicians, the military, and the people to work out. My interest was in keeping the Russians from doing harm to a defense program that had been planned and ordered by experts in Washington. Patriots like Charles Ajax.

It was nightfall when I came to the first fence surrounding a substation and the J-sector network of missiles. The fence was high, electrically-charged, and stretched away almost infinitely across the flat desert toward the high Pequop Mountains. I'd bought a small shovel in Wendover, at the town's only hardware store. I started digging a few feet away from the fence. The sand moved easily, and it took only ten minutes to learn that I couldn't dig my way in. A concrete footer, much like those used under the foundations of houses, rode along under the fence.

I never found out how deep the footer went. It

would have taken ten men ten days to dig that far. And I knew that if I tried to short out the electrical current in the fence, the action would show up on a computer readout screen in the nearby substation. There was no normal way over or through the fence.

I could have pole vaulted it if there had been a pole around, or even a tree tall enough to make into a pole. But the desert was full of only sagebrush, cactus, and twisted trees.

A brilliant idea came as I gazed at the sand I'd piled up.

I took the shovel and began digging again. I piled sand alongside the fence in an ever-rising heap. I packed it down by running up and down it, stomping with my shoes. When the pile was six feet high, and the clock had moved toward two in the morning, I figured it was high enough.

I backed the rented car up on the pile until the rear bumper was almost touching the fence. I climbed on top of the car and, voilá, there I was within inches of the top. I drove the car off the pile, heaped more and more sand on it, then tried it again.

This time, I was high enough to jump over without touching the electrified wires. The only trouble was that the fall down the other side was close to twelve feet. I could break both legs, among other things, in a jump from that height. The only thing going for me was the fact that the desert floor was sandy and soft.

Another brilliant idea.

It took another twenty minutes, but I kept hauling shovel loads of sand up and tossing them over the fence. When I had a nice, neat pile of loose sand on my chosen landing spot, I tossed over the shovel and leaped.

The sand broke my fall and not my legs. I was momentarily stunned and my side wound was complaining like hell, but I was inside the compound.

It was eerie walking across that forbidden territory. About a mile inside the fence, I came to freshly-dug dirt, indicating a tunnel. I followed the wide furrow and came to a cluster of low buildings. It was the J-Sector substation. About fifty feet to the left of the buildings were two vehicles, a dilapidated pickup truck and an old brown Chevrolet. I knew the substation was manned by a few technicians, that these were their cars. I had nothing to fear from the technicians. I would play my role to perfection.

I knocked on the door of the largest building, figuring it to be the computer control room. I heard rustling inside and the door opened. A young man with horn-rimmed glasses peered out at me. Beyond him was a soft blue light from a computer readout screen at work. I slapped open my wallet. On the inside leather was a Treasury Department badge I'd picked up years ago. It was big, it was gold, it had an American eagle on it, and it looked so damned official that the young technician nearly leaped to attention.

"Carter," I said, "from the office of Mr. Ajax. The boss is antsy about a Soviet spy known to be nosing about. Just checking to make sure everything is okay here."

"Yes, it's—I mean, yes, sir, everything is just fine. No trouble. Normal as apple pie."

"Where you from, son?"

"Nebraska."

"Thought so. You have that nice melodic ring to your voice. What's your name?"

He puffed up with pride, unaware that his nasal twang made my teeth hurt.

"Roger Wheaton," he said. He very nearly saluted, but didn't, adding "Sir," instead.

"Well, Mr. Wheaton, I'm afraid I'll have to ask you to open the locks and let me below for a few minutes. If you like, you can wake up one of the other techs and come along with me."

"Oh no, sir," he blustered. "That won't be necessary. I trust you. After all, you're from Mr. Ajax's office."

Poor sap.

"Mr. Wheaton, you know that and I know that, but the fact is I don't think you should let anyone —not even Mr. Ajax himself—go down into those tunnels without an official escort. Now, please wake up one of your buddies and have him man the screens while you and I take a little inspection tour."

I had good reason to want him along. I knew absolutely nothing about what was going on below. I needed a guide, although I didn't even know what I was looking for. I guess I needed to see for myself just how vulnerable our newest missile system might be to a man like Martin Steel.

Five minutes later, a sleepy young technician without horn-rimmed glasses was manning the computers and young Roger Wheaton and I were descending through the desert floor on a noisy, clanking elevator. I was surprised at the depth of the tunnels. I guessed our drop at three hundred feet, possibly much more since it was impossible to gauge the speed of that clanking elevator.

If the depth had surprised me, what I saw when

we emerged from the elevator literally jolted me. We were standing in a cavern that made the Holland Tunnel look like the inside of a finger from a very small glove. Six sets of tracks lined the floor of that vast tunnel. Lights stretched away into unfathomable distances in either direction. Somewhere in that great distance was a hollow roar, like a train rolling across a distant prairie.

I hid my shock well and looked at my watch. "What times does the next payload come by?"

He looked shocked. "Sir, nobody knows that. I thought you knew . . ."

"Of course, I know," I snapped, winking at him. "The hardware moves randomly according to the whim of the computer. I was just testing you."

He breathed a sigh of relief, knowing he'd passed the test. I also breathed a sigh of relief. I, too, had passed a test. I'd been guessing at the random movement being controlled by computer, and he'd confirmed my guess. I decided not to test the boy too rigidly. I might fail.

What was most obvious to me was that the wrong person in this vast network of tunnels could literally lose himself and do all sorts of damage. A bomb laid alongside a track, to be triggered by the next missile that randomly came along, would do a nasty trick and upset a lot of topsoil. Christ, a whole regiment of spies could roam these tunnels and never be spotted. Unless . . .

I tried one more test.

"Has your readout shown any foreign activity in or around these tunnels?"

"No, sir. Nothing. Not even a jackrabbit could get from this substation to the next without us knowing about it."

I breathed easier. For two reasons. One, I'd

passed another test, in spite of my ignorance. Two, it wasn't likely that Russian spies could wander at will among these tunnels. I felt better about both. Yet, something kept niggling at me. Martin Steel was out here—or had been out here—in advance of his inspection team. Why? What did he have in his little pea brain? What did the team members have in theirs?

I was about to ask how foolproof the system of detecting foreign objects in the tunnel system was when the distant roar suddenly became an earth-shaking tremor. The roar became much louder. For an instant I had no idea what was happening, and the surprise showed vividly on my face. Fortunately, Roger Wheaton was looking up the tracks and didn't see. Then, I saw it.

Great God, it was huge. It was so high that its shiny metal topside almost scraped the roof of the tunnel. It was so wide that the railroad caisson on which it rode took up three of the six sets of tracks on the tunnel floor.

The nose cone was about the size of a ship's bow and it widened out to a long, round cylinder that could have been the upper twenty floors of the Empire State Building.

I'd known these suckers were monstrous, but seeing one coming toward me down that badly-lighted tunnel, rumbling along like a traveling earthquake, shocked me so much that my mouth literally dropped open. Roger Wheaton backed away toward the elevator and I moved with him. I guessed that he was backing up to avoid a wind-draft sucking him beneath the wheels of that behemoth, but I was wrong. It was a gesture of politeness, of respect, the way a man might step back and tip his hat to the most beautiful girl in town when she sashays by.

This slow-rolling monster was in no hurry to get where it was going. At a given signal, it could stop, raise right up through the top of the tunnel, pushing away tons of desert, then fire its payload at a preordained target halfway across the world.

And there was nobody to say it nay.

Except perhaps Minya Stalin/Martin Steel.

When the missile was gone, I went back topside with Roger Wheaton, thanked him for his mini-tour, and asked him to let me through the gate. He looked puzzled, even a bit worried.

"Sir, I've been meaning to ask you just how you got in here without it showing on the computer readout?"

Well, he'd finally asked a question I couldn't answer. I thought of all sorts of cockamamie excuses, but none fit. Finally, I relied on the old AXE gambit of total secrecy.

"If I told you that, Mr. Wheaton," I said, my forefinger to my lips to bring him into my little conspiracy, "the enemy would love to be within earshot. The truth is, we have to have a system of penetration without detection. My driver stayed outside, so there's no breach of security. No harm done. I'd just as soon not use my penetration system going out. You understand."

He didn't, but he wasn't about to admit to any ignorance. He merely winked and said, "Sure enough, Sir. Happy to have had you aboard. Come back anytime."

And he went to the computer controls to unlatch the gate as I hot-footed it away in the darkness. Trouble was, I wasn't sure where the gate was. I found tire tracks, followed them and, sure enough, the gate was there. It opened to my touch and I took off at a dead run toward the pile of dirt where I'd left the rented car.

It was a three-mile run along the fence and I was beat when I reached the car. I sat behind the wheel, catching my wind, then drove down off the home-made hill and set a bearing for Wendover.

I was just crossing the Utah border, south of Wendover, when it all hit the fan. The road cut through the final pass in the foothills and I instinctively inspected the barren knolls on either side of the road. I saw the shadow, but it was too late.

I was already in his sights.

The first burst of the AK47 would have taken my head off if I hadn't seen that shadow. But I was already twisting the wheel of the car and dropping my body across the seat when Martin Steel pulled the trigger.

The spray of bullets caught the left side of the car just before I plowed the grille into the embankment on the right side of the road. I skittered across the seat, opened the passenger door, and did a flip-flop out into the rocky ditch.

This time, there was no tak-tak-tak-tak-tak sound. My executioner was closer than he'd been back in that Washington gorge, and the sound of that Russian weapon was more like PA-PA-PA-PA-POW. That horrifying sound filled the air in the narrow pass and damned near blew my eardrums inward.

Martin Steel was pulverizing the car, certain that I was still in it. Fragments of glass and steel and copper and lead showered me as I crawled up the side of the rocky butte. Once more, I was heading toward my assailant, not away from him. This time, I was certain, he wouldn't expect it. The side of the pass was like the side of a granite building.

Fear and adrenalin helped. I managed to find handholds. There weren't many. I found energy that I know had been expended in that run from the compound gate to the car. I found courage that only the most highly qualified fools are entitled to.

Just as my fingers stretched out and reached the top of the rocky knoll, the firing of the AK47 stopped. I figured Martin Steel would then go down and inspect what he hoped would be my bloody, bullet-riddled body. I waited, heard footsteps crunching above me, listened as they went past. I waited another few seconds, then pulled myself up.

My head cleared the top of the butte and I saw him standing just down the hill. He wore khakis and he held the AK47 at hip level. It was pointed at me.

I let go with both hands, hoping for gravity to drop me out of sight before he pulled that trigger.

Too late.

Even as my head was dropping past the edge of the ledge, the gun went off. Stone and dirt kicked up in front of my eyes. I felt the hammerblow of a slug against my skull, about three inches above my right eye.

It caught me a good one.

I felt my head snap back even as my body was free-falling back down toward the demolished car. I vaguely remember hitting the rocky ditch below, after a fifteen-foot fall. I seem to recall hearing the crunch of footsteps coming down the back side of the knoll and creeping up alongside the road.

And I also recall the hard muzzle of the AK47 turning me over. I could sense Martin Steel's eyes above me, watching for any sign of life.

Lucky for me, the fall had knocked all the breath out of me. I was so close to unconsciousness that I really didn't feel anything. No pain, no fear, no concern for what this killer might do next.

What he did next, I really don't know. I went unconscious and came to just as dawn was creeping down through the pass. Martin Steel hadn't made certain of my death. He hadn't emptied a clip into my unconscious body. It sure as hell wasn't out of compassion. His ego had ruled him, told him that his one clear shot at my head had done the trick.

To tell the truth, it almost had. Although the bullet obviously hadn't penetrated my skull and blown out my brains, it had knocked my skull out of shape so much that it was pressing on my brain, making me just as good as crazy.

I had no idea where I was or where I was supposed to go. I got up, as any wounded animal would, and began to walk.

I was walking westward, away from the rising sun. Wendover was east and north. Westward, there was nothing for miles and miles but desert and salt flats and jackrabbits and horribly twisted trees.

There was nothing at all out there, as far as I knew.

TEN

His name was Rain Allison, and he was a full-blooded Apache. He lived in a homemade adobe hut on just about the most barren stretch of desert this side of the Sahara. He drove a pickup truck that might have been traded in by Methuselah, smelled like a goat in heat and was infested with fleas from his thirteen dogs and seven goats.

But he was a savior in white as far as I was concerned. A knight in shining armor. A Samaritan, an angel, a Father Protector. He had a wide smile with bright shining teeth and when he used it, the sun got brighter in envy. Even on cloudy days.

I saw that brilliant smile when I first opened my eyes. What had brought me around was the jostling and rattling of the pickup truck, although I didn't know at the time that I was anything but a piece of dead wood on the desert floor.

"Hey, welcome back, old buddy," he said through that bright smile. "Glad to see you're worth my trouble."

It was my turn, finally, to say: "Who are you?"

And he told me. He was twenty-eight years old. His parents had died in Idaho fifteen years ago and he'd come to poach on this open desert as a child.

"I make a little whiskey from the corn I grow, sell it in Wendover, buy dogfood for the dogs I pick up as strays, mind my own business, take a bath once every change of seasons, and read Plato when I can't afford a good dirty magazine from the drugstore in Wendover."

He chatted on about himself as he lifted me, like a rag doll, from the bed of the pickup truck and took me into his dark, smelly hut. He chatted as he put something warm and sticky and incredibly smelly on my head wound. He chatted even after I fell asleep from the drug he gave me from a gourd shell he used as a cup. I fell asleep wondering how such a dirty Indian in such a dirty house maintained such a fine set of gleaming white teeth.

I awoke to another dawn. Rain Allison was outside feeding his dogs and scratching fleas along with the best of them. I tried to remember where I was and all that Rain Allison had told me.

He'd mostly chatted about the wonderful loneliness of his desert life, how he'd once in a while drink some of the moonshine he made, how he'd fought a valiant battle against people who'd tried to chase him off the land, how he wanted no part of civilization, but managed (at each change of season) to find a woman to sleep with. Rain Allison was as scattered as I felt. And I felt pretty scattered.

"Hey, welcome back, old buddy," he said as he entered the hut and saw that my eyes were open. "Feel better? You ought to. That poultice I put on your head is made of genuine goat piss and dog turds and wild herbs. You feel like eating something?"

I looked at him, at that fine smile that had

brought sunshine into the hut. All I could think to say was:

"How do you keep your teeth so white?"

He laughed and slapped his thigh. I noticed that his ancient bluejeans were made up mostly of patches from other bluejeans and animal skins. His denim shirt had obviously been made the same year as his pickup truck, but was in worse shape. His long golden hair was as clean as his teeth. Jesus, talk about a man of serious contradictions.

"I eat cactus," he said. "That keeps 'em white and clean and as sweet-smelling as a woman's breasts. You want some cactus? Minus the needles, of course?"

"I'll eat anything," I said, remembering my usual breakfast diet of Wheaties, powdered milk, and frozen bread.

"Sit up," he said. "You're strong enough. Your head won't fall off. That poultice drew out the poison and pulled your skull away from your brain. You're as good as new, even if you don't feel like it."

I sat up. He was right. My head didn't fall off. It didn't even hurt. The man had worked a miracle, or the wound wasn't as bad as I'd figured. Memories came back. I saw Martin Steel standing on top of that butte, saw the tongue of flame, saw myself falling back into space, felt the hard muzzle of the gun turning my body over.

"Now," he said as I ate something gray and sticky and delicious from a gourd bowl, "tell me what happened."

I lied to the Indian and he knew I was lying. I said I worked for the government as a technician assigned to the missile program. I said a soldier

must have mistaken me for an intruder when I'd
gone on an inspection tour, had shot me and . . .
and the Indian stopped me.

"Forget I asked," he said, grinning, showing he
wasn't offended by my wild and obviously false
tale. "Eat and get well."

He got up and left. His dogs and goats followed,
yelping, bleating, scratching, snarling, and fighting
for position to be the closest to the master. I felt
rotten lying to the man. He was far too intelligent
to have swallowed that bunch of rot. But the truth
would have sounded even more rotten. And it
would have made no difference in my relationship
with this renegade Indian, this rugged individual.
Still, I felt bad. Physically, though, I felt great. I
got up and was surprised that I didn't feel dizzy.
My head still didn't hurt. My eyes were sharp and
clear. My mind functioned better than it had in
weeks. I mosied around the hut and, sure enough,
there were the complete works of Plato: *The Re-
public, The Apology, The Letters.* And all the rest of
the Dialogues: *Charmides, Crito, Euthyphro, Hip-
pias Minor, Ion, Laches, Lysis*—all of them. All
three groups, written at different periods of the
philosopher's life.

Right beside the works of Plato was a stack of
magazines. I checked the titles and recognized
none. I opened the pages and recognized instantly
what I saw. Closeups of women's genitals covered
all the pages. There were few words in the magazines. Actually, no words were needed.

Strange man, Rain Allison.

I went outside, feeling a little wobbly in the legs,
but still okay. Rain and his troop of dogs and goats
were down in a field where the Indian was tenderly

watering some tiny green shoots. I looked around and saw his well, surrounded by stones he'd gathered from the desert floor and hauled in here to keep the soft, sandy ground from caving into the water. There was an outhouse, just enough of a structure to keep rain and wind from blowing the user off the seat. There was a small adobe hut that looked like a smokehouse. I figured he had jackrabbits preserved in there for future meals. Or perhaps it was the storehouse for the goat piss, dog turds, and herbs he used in his poultices.

"Don't that sun feel wonderful?" Rain said as he and the animals came strolling up from the field.

He sat on a stone and motioned to another stone a few feet away. We sat there as the dogs and goats settled themselves like loyal subjects around Rain's feet. A couple of dogs started to fight for a better position. Rain stroked them gently; they were instantly at peace.

"You know," he said, gazing off toward the distant Pequop Mountains, "Plato once said that a man is happiest when he's ruled by the noblest elements in himself. I have a feeling, Mr. Nick Carter, that you are not a happy man. And it has nothing to do with what happened to you back there in that pass."

So, he had seen the bullet-riddled car, knew that I had been attacked by someone who knew me and was definitely out to kill me. I felt even more sheepish about the yarn I'd spun about the soldier mistaking me for an intruder.

Even worse, I was stung by that remark about the noblest elements. Was I guilty of letting myself be ruled by base, banal—even corrupt—elements? Was I devoid of any noble attributes? Possibly, but

I didn't like to think of myself that way.

"I learned many years ago," Rain continued, "to live by Plato's wisdom. You may think me weird because of my quaint habits, my choosing to live apart from others, my disobeyance of certain civilized rules, even my choice to ignore certain hygienic practices. And I'm sure you saw the books inside and think of me as some kind of pervert. Plato didn't have much to say about the female body, but Larry Flynt does. He said the female body is sweetest when man is ruled by passion. Taking that a step further, passion is a noble element, so Mr. Flynt and Plato aren't far apart in their individual philosophies. Now intelligence and wisdom are something else." He looked directly into my eyes and I saw that his were a shade of ocher, very deep, very sharp, like a desert sunrise. "You insulted my intelligence with your story. I won't ask you anything more about yourself. You're alive and you're mending fast. That's what's important. I do hope when you return to civilization that you'll think of what Plato said. And now, I have something else I want to discuss with you."

I shifted uneasily on the stone. He was hitting sensitive personal targets. I had the feeling that he was moving into an even more sensitive area.

"You mentioned the missile program," Rain said in his soft voice. "I won't get on my bandwagon or soap box, but you might as well know that I fought that program harder than I fought anything in my life. I lost, as you know, but I'm still thinking on it. If I find a way, I'll destroy that terrible violation of the land, of the planet, of man's noble elements."

"Why are you so against it? It doesn't even come near your little place in the sun here."

"When the bombs and missiles come from Russia," he said, "my little place in the sun will be a very large black smudge on the earth. It will be so highly radioactive that nothing will live here for ten thousand years. Not even the sweet cactus. Not even the fleas that keep me and my animals company day and night."

"You're probably right," I said. "I don't pretend to have the answers. I only know that Russia has built similar capabilities. I'm not worried about America's intentions on using its capabilities, but I am concerned about Russia's."

"A cop-out statement. You sound like that monster, Charles Ajax."

"What do you know about Charles Ajax?"

"Plenty. He's been here off and on for the past several years, selling people on his damned program. He was here just a few days ago and made a speech, got his picture in the paper. The most dangerous thing about Charles Ajax is that he's convinced he's right. A man like that finds it easier to convince others, sway them, lull them into a false sense of security. Frankly, old buddy, I hate the cocksucker. And he's different now. This last speech showed him as the true dictator he is—or would like to be. You know Charles Ajax?"

"No, but I've been looking for him. There's some information I have that he should know about."

Rain got up and went into the adobe hut. He came out with a fairly fresh newspaper, the Wendover *Bugle*. He spread it out and there was a picture of Charles Ajax giving his latest speech to a group of locals.

Something about the picture jarred me. I'd seen photos of Ajax before, in other newspapers. This was Ajax, all right, but there was something decidedly different about him. The eyes. They seemed to bore right into me. I was certain that I'd seen those eyes before. I couldn't place where. I shivered looking at those eyes.

"He's got a God complex," Rain said. "I fear all men who have God complexes. I think, Mr. Carter, that there are times when you play God."

Another raw target area. Yes, I played God each time I pulled Wilhelmina's trigger or slid Hugo around a vulnerable neck or dropped a lethal Pierre into a group of attackers. But it was also eliminating a threat, a matter of self-defense.

"Yes," I said. "There are many times I play God. I don't know if it's noble or not. But I don't have the philosophical mind of a Plato. I do what I've been trained to do, and I do it very well."

"You didn't do it so well in that pass. Some other trained ape did it better, except he forgot to finish you off."

This man was uncanny in his ability to figure things out for himself. I had the creepy feeling that he had, in his mind's eye, a true visual picture of what had happened in that pass south of Wendover.

"You win some, you lose some," I said. "If I stop to think too deeply about it, I'd start losing them all."

"So you won't think about it."

"No."

That was a lie. I thought about it a great deal. It was not coldness or brutality or lack of compassion that made me heave out my guts after killing that poor, fat, stupid Senator Lou Barker. In its own way, it was a noble element forcing its way to the surface.

"Yes, you will," Rain said, as though reading my mind. "I was too harsh on you when I said you weren't ruled by noble elements. It's just that your noble elements are different from mine. All right. *Noblesse oblige*. You do your thing, I'll do mine, and never the twain shall meet. Or fight. Go in peace, Mr. Carter. I've done all I can for you."

He used the term figuratively, of course. I stayed the day and night, and he drove me into Wendover the next morning. I still felt great. At the tiny airport, where I'd catch the commuter flight back to Vegas and make connections for Denver and Washington—off to try to find Charles Ajax—he gripped my hand with firmness and gazed deeply into my eyes.

"Plato also said, in effect, that until philosophers are kings, and political authority and wisdom are united in one, cities will never have rest from their troubles—no, nor the human race."

I grinned back at him.

"Any final word from Larry Flynt?"

"No, but one from me. At least once a season, take yourself a bath and lie with a good woman. It will improve your skills, even killing skills, immensely."

"Good advice," I said and said goodbye. I didn't have the heart to tell him I had been living by that code for years. And my seasons were much shorter in duration than his.

He stayed at the airport and waved as the plane made a circle and headed southwest, toward Las Vegas. I thought wistfully, if all goes rotten in my chosen profession someday, I might be inclined to go back to that desert hovel and live out my days with a man like Rain Allison.

I truly envied him. Fleas and all.

Felicia was waiting for me in the apartment. She'd indeed done some grocery shopping. She fixed us a fine meal of porterhouse steak, baked potatoes with sour cream, a marvelous salad and strawberry shortcake. We made love before and after the meal, and it was definitely sweet because we were both ruled by passion.

Felicia fretted over my head wound, but I wouldn't let her remove the smelly poultice Rain Allison had put on it. There was still no pain and my mind was sharp and clear. I would leave well enough alone.

"But that awful stuff he put in it," she complained, holding her nose. "My God, you could get all sorts of infections in your brain."

"That kind of infection I can live with. Have you given further thought to finding friends to help us crack this case? We have only a little time before the Russians arrive."

"Wrong," she said, "we have *no* time. There was a story in today's paper. They arrived last night and are billeted at Fort Belvoir over in Virginia. The American inspection team has left for Russia, but the actual inspections won't start for a couple of days."

"Then it's even more important that I meet with Charles Ajax. I don't think he was in Utah at the headquarters, but I don't know for certain. I have to find out."

I called his home, got the same pitch from the servant with the accent. Mr. Ajax was out of town and Mrs. Ajax was sleeping. At nine o'clock in the evening. I called his office and an aide told me the boss was out of town. This time I decided to leave a message.

"Tell him that Nick Carter wants to meet him on an urgent matter. In case he doesn't know, Nick Carter is the man who killed Senator Barker, Allen Pierson, Donald Stanton, and Leland Hutchings. I'm certain he knows they were killed and didn't die of heart attacks. You tell him that and I'll call back in three minutes."

I called back in four minutes. Charles Ajax came immediately to the phone, demanding to know the whole story.

"Not over the phone," I said. "We'll have to meet in person." I had to meet with him face to face, to see those eyes, to eliminate or confirm the crazy feeling I'd had when I'd looked at that photo of him in the Wendover *Bugle*.

All right. Come to my office in twenty minutes."

"Not hardly," I said. "I'm a wanted man, you know. You leave your office and head down Pennsylvania Avenue past the Capitol Building. Stop at the corner of Pennsylvania and D Street. There's a phone booth there. When it rings, answer it. And come alone."

I hung up and looked across at Felicia. She was curled up on the couch sipping brandy she'd also bought. I had only Scotch in the apartment for sipping purposes.

"He won't come alone, you know."

"I know."

I checked Wilhelmina and tried the trigger release on Hugo a couple of times. I got out a harmless nerve-gas Pierre and a lethal Pierre. I went into the bathroom, snuggled the lethal bomb in its pouch behind my testicles, but put the harmless one in my jacket pocket. If Ajax came with the Russian dull-suiters who'd taken Felicia for such a merry ride, I'd use the one in the sheath. If FBI or other American law-enforcement people showed up, I'd merely put them to sleep.

If I got the chance.

"I have to get there first and copy down the number in that phone booth," I told Felicia. "I'll lead him a merry chase and wind up at . . ."

"Don't tell me," she said, pursing her lips over the snifter. "If anything goes wrong, I don't want you suspecting me."

"Right. Well, see you later."

"Maybe you will, maybe you won't."

"What's that supposed to mean?"

With a sob, she put down the brandy snifter and leaped from the chair. She came into my arms, kissed my lips and cheeks and forehead. She didn't seem to mind the stinking poultice.

"I have such a bad feeling about all this," she said. "I don't want you to go. I'm afraid you . . ."

"Won't come out of it alive? Don't worry. I think Charles Ajax is the only man in Washington we can trust." I was lying, and she knew it.

"I still have a bad feeling."

"Sweetheart," I said, going to the door and turning the knob, "I have that feeling every time I step out into the streets. See you later."

And I was gone. I took Felicia Starr's bad feeling with me. It wasn't her bad feeling exclusively. I'd had it from the time I saw that newspaper photo Rain Allison had shown me. The one of Charles Ajax—with those familiar eyes.

But I had to go. Noble elements told me to.

ELEVEN

I made a quick run down Pennsylvania Avenue, around the Capitol, and stopped a half block down from D Street. I ran back to the phone booth on the corner, copied down the number, ran back to the car and sped on down Pennsylvania to its juncture with Kentucky Avenue, near the approach to John Philip Sousa Memorial Bridge.

After getting the number of a phone in a booth there, I backtracked up Kentucky to Lincoln Park, at East Capitol Street. I got the number in one of a dozen booths there, then blasted off down East Capitol all the way to 19th Street, S. E.

Ahead, D. C. Stadium, home of the Redskins, loomed like some sleeping monster. Beyond it were the Anacostia River and the East Capitol Street Bridge. There were two vast parking lots on either side of the stadium. I chose the one on the right and turned off my headlights as I drove across it, snuggled up against the stadium under a kind of portico roof, and got out. I went to a bank of phone booths alongside the steel fencing that kept spectators from just wandering into the empty stadium.

The sound of my footsteps echoed through the

open steel fence, into the vast chasm that was the stadium. The sound was eerie, haunting. The echo, like the ghost of some great athlete stomping through time, came back through the gridwork of steel and dissipated itself across the dark, empty parking lot.

I was ready to start making my calls now, start Charles Ajax on a quick but out-of-the-way trip from that phone booth on Pennsylvania Avenue and D Street to this lonely parking lot at D. C. Stadium.

This was to be our meeting ground, though I entertained no illusions that he would come alone. Of course he'd have some kind of backup. I was curious to see if the backup consisted of FBI men or the Russian circus act that had done such a bad job of containing Felicia Starr.

Before picking up the receiver and depositing the coins, I checked the two versions of Pierre. Which would I be forced to use tonight, the good one or the lethal one?

Of course, there was the distinct possibility that Charles Ajax, fearing no man because of his own vast importance, would come alone. I hoped so. I wanted to meet him eyeball to eyeball. I wanted to tell him about the senator, about Pierson, Stanton, and Hutchings. Mostly, I wanted to tell him about his chief deputy, John Pesco, and the killer-spy known as Martin Steel.

Then to really shock him, I'd throw in names like Natoly Dobrinka, the Russian Embassy contact for all the traitors, and Harold Brookman, the biggest fish in the sea of treason that I'd caught up with so far. Harold Brookman, chief aide to the secretary of defense, technically the boss of Charles

Ajax. I wanted to see the missile program chief's peculiar but familiar eyes when I told him about Brookman, his boss, and how he was leading the pack of traitors.

He picked up the receiver at the Pennsylvania Avenue and D Street phone booth on the first ring. I kept silence for five seconds, waiting for the telltale click that would warn me if he'd brought along a technician to tape into the phone. He hadn't.

"Go to Pennsylvania and Kentucky Avenues," I said. "There are six phone booths on the circle near the approach to the Sousa Bridge. The third one from the west end will ring in precisely four minutes."

"I can't get there in four . . ."

I hung up, betting heavily that he would get there in four minutes. And he did. I timed my call precisely and the phone rang only twice when a breathless Charles Ajax answered.

"Head northwest now," I said, after waiting again for the click of the phone tap. "Go back up Kentucky Avenue to Lincoln Park. On the south side are a dozen phone booths. Go to the one on your right, the eastern side, and listen for the ring. It will come in three minutes."

"Jesus Christ," he bellowed into the phone. "You know it's impossible to get there in . . ."

It wasn't impossible, just difficult. I was betting heavily that he would pick up the phone by the third ring.

I lost. The damned thing rang six times before Charles Ajax moaned into the receiver: "Carter, give me a break. I'm not a young man anymore."

"I wasn't aware that you were pushing your

car," I said with flipness, "I thought you were driving it."

"Where to now?"

"Head out on East Capitol. At Nineteenth Street, you'll see one lonely phone booth. Sit down and wait. The call won't come for two minutes."

"Two what?"

I hung up. He had a five-minute drive under his belt, unless he drove like a maniac and crashed every red light. He obviously did both. He picked up the phone on the fourth ring. He was so out of breath, from jumping in and out of his car and racing to phone booths, that he could barely talk.

"Where . . . to . . . now?"

I thought of sending him on a merry chase back through the center of Washington, perhaps even as far back as the Lincoln Memorial, but I didn't have any phone numbers there for him to catch. I had no choice but to cut the guy some slack. If he had men to back him up, and if they'd kept pace, I'd know it soon enough. If not, we'd finally have that eyeball-to-eyeball meeting I'd been hankering for ever since I'd learned that his chief deputy was a traitor.

"Drive into D. C. Stadium, into the parking lot on the right. Park in the center of the lot and go to the phonebooth near Gate C. Take the second booth from the left."

And here is where I made my mistake. I forgot to tell him how long he had to answer. I knew he had reached his final destination, but he didn't. My mistake told him, though. He knew now. There was almost a lilt in his voice when he asked:

"How long do I have to get there?"

I tried to recover. "It's just a hop, skip, and a

jump from where you are now. I'll give you a full minute."

But he knew. He would know that I was in that parking lot, probably in another booth. He would be looking for my car. I quickly left the booth and drove the car farther around the wall of the oval-shaped stadium. I dashed back to the booth, took out the lightbulb, and closed the door. Then, I backed away into the shadows and waited.

Not a moment too soon. Headlights of a slow-moving car eased into the parking area. I stepped behind a circular column when the lights swept over my way. The car stopped about fifty feet from the line of phone booths and I knew he was watching the booth with the door closed, figuring that I was in there.

The minute went past and nobody emerged from the car. I started getting antsy, but knew it would be a mistake to move from my position. But that damned phone wasn't ringing as it was supposed to. Charles Ajax had used my own mistake to fake me out.

Before I could decide on a move, a whole line of cars came screeching into the parking lot, headlights and spotlights glaring. I moved farther into the darkness, but the lights found me as the cars went for various positions in the lot, triangulating their headlights in the vicinity of the phone booths.

Men poured from the six cars and knelt on the asphalt with pistols drawn and pointed. They were all pointed at me. I stood out in the glaring light like a performer on a stage.

"FBI," a voice roared through a bullhorn. "Come forward ten paces, Mr. Carter, or we'll blow you away."

There were perhaps twenty guns leveled at me, all .38 specials, government issue. I felt better about Charles Ajax—at least he hadn't brought Russians. That proved nothing, but I did feel better. But I was pissed off at myself for blowing the deal.

If Ajax had come expecting to be sent to another location, his backup units wouldn't have arrived so soon. I'd have had at least a minute or two to talk with him, to see him, to satisfy myself that Charles Ajax was not a traitor.

Now, I had no choice but to walk the ten paces forward. It would put me to within twenty feet of his car and perhaps I'd get a glimpse of him.

That wasn't to be. I'd walked only four paces when the car bearing Charles Ajax backed up and made a violent, screeching turn in the parking area. The car streaked out of the lot and back into the Washington streets.

The FBI men swarmed around me. One of them took out handcuffs, but another shook his head. With such an escort, why use cuffs?

"You're to come with us, Sir," a young, stocky, clean-shaven agent said. "Give us no trouble and we'll give you none. Take the car just ahead of you. Walk slowly."

I walked slowly. As soon as I was past the glare of the headlights, and could feel the whole gang of them all around me, I slipped my hand into my jacket pocket and pulled the pin on Pierre—the one with the nerve gas. Or, so I hoped. If I'd made another mistake and gotten them switched, I'd *really* be a fugitive from justice.

It's not easy for anyone, even a Killmaster for AXE, to justify the killing of twenty agents of the

Federal Bureau of Investigation. No matter what the reason.

I took a deep breath, knowing I had to hold it for nearly two full minutes until the gas had dissipated in the calm night air. I dropped the little bomb to the ground, stepped into the car and closed the door.

I still held my breath, just in case some of the nerve gas seeped into the car. I watched, fascinated as the FBI men dropped, by twos and threes, like fallen leaves around a very bright tree.

It was all over in thirty seconds, but I still held my breath. I looked out at the sleeping bodies, started the car, backed gingerly through the fallen agents and drove out of the lot, onto East Capitol Street. I drove slowly, in no hurry now because I had no one to meet, no one to talk to. It would be useless to call Charles Ajax again. It would also be useless to stay on the streets. In an hour, the FBI men would be awake, and madder than hornets.

Once they reported back what had happened, every law enforcement agent in the city would be after me.

My only recourse was to return to the apartment and tell Felicia how I'd botched the meeting and made myself an even greater target for both sides of the fence—Americans and Russians alike.

I made one stop, at Lincoln Park. I used the same phone booth Charles Ajax had used, smelled a familiar scent, and called Hawk at home.

"Nick, you're getting in deeper and deeper," he said after I'd told him of my latest escapade. "The Russian inspection team is here and ours will arrive in Moscow within the hour. If you only knew how your activities are upsetting a very sensitive and delicate situation. How can I get through to you?"

"By telling me the truth," I said.

"I'll tell you this," he said. "We know of Martin Steel's presence in the U. S. We know it has something to do with the inspection team. But we have all bases covered."

"Why hasn't there been any publicity about my kills, about the traitors I've taken out?"

"Nick, if the public knew that treason existed in the missile program, the program and the inspection effort would be scrapped. You know how difficult a time Congress had approving that program. There was intense pressure from citizens, from lobbying groups. If the public knew what was happening now, there could be a grass-roots uprising against the program. Not only would billions of dollars go down the drain, but we'd fall far behind the Russians in defense capabilities. That's why your activities are upsetting things. Charles Ajax has so far been able to cover your tracks and keep things from the news media. But he can only do so much. Sooner or later . . ."

"Sooner or later," I interrupted, "the truth has to be told. You say you're on top of things. Do you know that an imposter entered the J-Sector missile substation in Utah a few nights ago, went below to inspect the tunnel, and actually saw a missile ride by on its tracks?"

"Where did you get that information?"

"I didn't get it. I made it. I was the imposter."

"Nick, you fool. You have to stop what you're doing. You have to give yourself up as the President has ordered. You have to . . ."

"I'm not really listening, Sir," I said. "I'll listen when you tell me why you lied about being in my

hospital room the night I was shot by Martin
Steel."

"I wasn't lying," he said, his voice a deep and
anguished plea. "I was *not* in your hospital room.
I knew nothing of the incident until you told me
about it. And that is the truth, Nick."

And I believed him. Somehow I knew he was
telling the truth. Then who the hell was in that
room, looking down at me, shaking his head, gripping his cigar in his teeth.

I suddenly had a thought. Perhaps not a brilliant
one, but at least a thought. There was something I
had to check out.

"Goodbye, Sir," I said.

"Nick, please turn yourself in at FBI headquarters. Or come to me. I'll . . ."

I hung up. That thought, brilliant or not, was
growing into a compulsion.

I raced to the vicinity of my apartment in the
FBI car. I parked the car in front of Blair House
and didn't leave my CIA card on the windshield.
Let the cops haul it away, let the FBI figure out
what had happened to it. I walked from there to
my apartment. It wasn't all that far.

Felicia heard my story, nodding all the way as
though she'd expected no less. What had happened
to her great feeling of foreboding? Was she losing
faith in me since I didn't come back with another
gunshot wound for her to tend?

"I'd try once again to get some allies from your
contacts and mine," I said, "but there's no time.
I've got to get to the bottom of this mystery before
that Russian team arrives at the missile site."

"What are you going to do next?"

"Do you really want to know?"

"No. Will it be dangerous?"

"Not likely. The dead are rarely dangerous."

I left her puzzling over that one and went back to Blair House to see if the FBI car was still there. I decided to make use of it as long as its agent-owner was probably still snoozing away out at the home of the Redskins. The car was there. I started it, made a U-turn and raced east again, this time heading for the City Morgue, nestled between the Congressional Cemetery and D. C. General Hospital.

I'd always thought that a cozy but ghoulish arrangement—a morgue sandwiched between a hospital and a cemetery. But I suppose it was merely practical. There were funeral homes in the area, too.

I used the old Treasury badge bit to get cooperation from the guard. He was a sleepy-looking old codger who probably kept his civil service job out of tenure. He certainly didn't earn it from his energy and devotion to his job.

"A man was fished out of the river about five days ago," I told him. "We haven't identified him yet, but I want to have another look."

I knew the system. Unidentified bodies were sometimes buried by welfare funds in three or four days. Bodies that revealed any sign of importance (gold fillings, clean fingernails, pampered bodies) were kept on refrigeration for as long as a month. I had a feeling that this body had all three requirements for a long stay on ice.

"Down there," the guard said without leaving his comfortable seat in the marble foyer. "Take that door on your right, go down one flight. Open the door with the window in it. The body is in the third tier on your left, bottom drawer.

"Okay. Thanks for all your help."

He missed the facetious tone, sank into a civil service stupor, and I followed his directions to a tee.

There is something even less palatable about a body in a morgue than one lying on a sidewalk in a pool of blood. The cyanosed pallor of the skin is enough to make your own skin crawl. The slack, swollen features look as though they've never had anything to do with a living being. Bodies in morgues give me the creeps, and I've seen a lot of bodies in morgues.

I slid the tray open slowly. It moved on well-lubricated wheels, even though the steel slab on which the body lay was heavy as hell. The feet came first. A tag was tied to the man's right big toe. There was a number and a location on it: 37622, 400 yds. s.e. of T. Roosevelt Bridge, west Potomac shore, State of Virginia.

I opened the tray farther. There was a gaping wound in the chest. The man had obviously been shot several times in one place, possibly with an automatic weapon. An AK47? And he's obviously been thrown from the Theodore Roosevelt Bridge and had drifted downstream to the Virginia side, directly across the river from the Lincoln Memorial.

I had no idea what the number, 37622 meant. Perhaps there'd been that many bodies fished from the river since Washington became a city. It was a possibility. But I did know that this was the body mentioned in the newspaper the morning I was looking for news of my bloody kills. And he wasn't a senator.

When I got to the face, the electric shock that wracked my body made my own skin take on a cyanosed pallor.

I knew that face, swollen as it was. I'd seen pictures of it in newspapers. I'd seen a picture of it just recently, in the adobe hut of an Indian named Rain Allison.

And yet, it wasn't the same man. It couldn't be.

If hunch, instinct, and memory served me right, this was the body of Charles Ajax!

But Charles Ajax was very much alive. He'd made a speech in Wendover, Utah, just a few days ago. I'd talked to him on the phone several times this evening.

And, if this body was that of Charles Ajax, why was it still listed as unidentified?

Most of the people in Washington would recognize him instantly. I didn't like what I was starting to think. My mind was seeing a pair of eyes in eight photos David Hawk had shown me from AXE files, and in the photo Rain Allison had shown me.

A pattern was developing, my hunch deepening. I had to learn the truth.

And damned quick.

TWELVE

The home of Charles Ajax was located in the Queens Chapel Manor section, across the Anacostia River in Maryland. It was a modest house in comparison to John Pesco's house, the house of Charles Ajax's chief deputy. It didn't make sense.

I wasted no time. I parked a block from the house and walked the dark street up to the front door. I rang the bell and fished around for my wallet for the phony Treasury Department badge.

A hulking giant of a man in butler garb answered the door. I didn't even have to hear him talk to know that he spoke with an accent, that he'd been the man who'd answered the phone each time I'd called here.

"Yes. What do you want?" he demanded.

Definitely an Eastern European accent. Possibly Russian. But I wouldn't jump to conclusions.

"I'd like to speak with Mrs. Ajax," I said, slapping open the wallet.

The man didn't even look at the badge.

"Not here," he belched.

"Where is she? I have some disturbing news about her husband. It's imperative that I see her, speak with her."

"In Paris," the butler said. "She went to Paris, France, early this morning. Won't be back for maybe two to three months."

I could have disabled the bastard and searched the house for myself, but I wasn't all that certain of my hunches. The body in the morgue could have been someone whose features vaguely resembled Charles Ajax. I had the man so much on the brain that my eyes could be playing tricks on me. And I was in more trouble than I could handle from barging headlong into my own little projects.

"Can you give me the name of her hotel in Paris?" I said.

"She stays with friends," he said, without batting an eye. He had it all down pat. Or he was telling the truth. "Not to be disturbed."

"Yes," I said. "It figures. Tell me, what flight did she take to Paris?"

"No more talk," he said. "Mrs. Ajax not to be disturbed."

He slammed the door and I toyed with the idea of kicking it down and taking that Russian butler apart bit by bit.

If only I could have been certain.

I backed off the porch, sat in the car thinking for a time, then went to a drugstore. There was a friend in the State Department I could trust, at least to do a little digging.

I called Henry Riddle, a man just as strange and enigmatic as his name. "I want you to do some checking for me, Hank. Mrs. Charles Ajax, first name, Henriette, is supposed to have left for Paris early today. I need her passport number."

I gave him the drugstore telephone to call, then called a friend at TWA.

"Bill, I need a favor. Check all flights on all airlines for Paris since midnight yesterday. I want to know if a Mrs. Charles Ajax or a Mrs. Henriette Ajax was on one of those flights. No questions, buddy. Just call me back at 555-1212 when you have the data."

I hung up before he could remind me that I was asking the impossible. Bill of TWA might not know that I was a fugitive, but I was certain that Henry Riddle of the State Department knew. But neither man would question my requests. They owed me big favors.

Results weren't long in coming. I was on my second cup of coffee and wanting to call Felicia just to hear her voice when the pay phone rang. I winked at the clerk and answered. It was Bill from TWA.

"She didn't go to Paris under either name," he said. "Got another name for me to check?"

"Santa Claus," I joked, "but he has his own private airline and we can't check it out. Thanks. You still owe me."

He groaned and I hung up. The phone rang again the minute I broke the connection. It was Henry Riddle.

"I can't give you a passport number for Mrs. Charles Ajax," he said, "because she doesn't have one. The woman is deathly afraid of airplanes and ships, and hates foreign countries anyway. The word I get is that she's kind of a recluse. Never goes out of the house. There are a lot of people with phobias like that. Henriette Ajax is one of them."

All right. It was decided. I had to get into the Ajax house. I wouldn't try to go through that burly Russian butler. I'd wait until all the lights were out and go in surreptitiously. I had a pretty good idea that the woman was being hidden away in a bedroom.

But she had to leave that house. She had to go with me to the D. C. Morgue, to tell me if the hunk of meat on that cold slab was her husband or someone who looked like him.

I didn't have long to wait. The lights didn't go off, but something I should have anticipated came down.

I was sitting there, slouched in the seat, running my fingers over the stinking poultice Rain Allison had put on my head, when I felt something hard against my left temple.

"Don't turn, don't move, don't shout," a calm, cool, steely voice said. "You're covered from both sides."

With peripheral vision, I saw the man with the gun on my left. And I saw two men with guns move up to the open window on the right. Damn summer, I thought. If it had been a cold winter night, I'd have had the windows up and the motor running. I might have made a fast getaway.

As it was, I didn't turn, didn't move, didn't shout. I just sat there as a dozen FBI agents rousted me from the car, handcuffed me, and shoved me into the back seat of another car.

"Listen to me," I said as the car sped away from the quiet street. "There's something you people have to know. Charles Ajax is dead and on a slab down at . . ."

"Don't talk," the man on my right commanded. "We don't want to hear."

The man on my left in the tightly-packed rear seat gave an "amen" to that.

"Dammit, you have to hear. You . . ."

"Our orders are clear, Mister Carter," the man on my left said. "You could tell us you were God. You could even perform a couple of bona fide miracles. We'd still follow orders. You know that."

Yeah, I knew that. But I wished to hell I'd had a couple of miracles to pull off. Not to prove anything to these non-listening automatons, but to make them disappear, along with the damned handcuffs that were already turning my wrists into raw meat.

There were two cars of agents in front of us, one in the rear. I had no miracles at hand. And they'd taken Wilhelmina and Hugo from me. I still had Pierre in his little pouch behind my testicles, but there was no way I'd use that lethal weapon against these guys. Even with the windows open, I'd die with them.

I tried to lean back and relax, to enjoy the rape, so to speak. There was no relaxing. I was sitting on those damned handcuffs that had my wrists in a stranglehold.

"Just for the hell of it," I said, using a light, genial tone, "where are you taking me?"

"You'll know when you get there," said the man on my left.

I soon had the answer to my question, I knew as soon as the FBI cars eased onto the I-395 Innerbelt highway in Virginia. We were heading for Fort Belvoir.

It was as Hawk had said. Once I was arrested, I'd be taken to Fort Belvoir and kept incommunicado by military police until the missile site inspections were over. Then the President would decide what to do about prosecuting me for the "murders."

But a ray of hope crept in when I realized that we were really going to Fort Belvoir. Felicia had learned that the Russian inspection team had already arrived and was at Fort Belvoir. They planned to leave at dawn tomorrow.

Was it fate that was putting me in the same location as the inspection team?

If so, how did fate expect to get me out of these handcuffs and away from the military police to do anything about it?

The truth was, fate had nothing to do with it. The chances of me getting away and learning anything more than I already knew about Charles Ajax and the Russian inspection team were slimmer than they'd ever been.

If the FBI men would only listen.

I tried again to tell them that I was convinced that Charles Ajax was dead, that someone was taking his place. I had a fair hunch as to who that someone was, but I had no proof of anything.

"Stow it," the man on my left said. "I told you . . ."

"Yeah, I know. Even if I were God and performed a couple of miracles, you still would follow orders. Well maybe I can convince someone when we get to Fort Belvoir."

The agent on my left and the agent on my right threw quick glances at me, surprised that I'd guessed the destination. I didn't tell them that it was no guess, that I'd been forewarned of this fate.

Let the damned automatons think I'd just performed my first miracle.

They were very thorough in their search at the military guardhouse in Fort Belvoir. The FBI agents turned me over to a squad of big, tough-looking marine guards. These honorable guardians of the peace took me into a bare room, stripped off all my clothes, found Pierre nestled behind my testicles, removed the weapon, and continued the search until all of my outside and a fair portion of my inside had been thoroughly examined.

And then they hustled me into another room where a doctor took a fluoroscope of me to make certain I hadn't swallowed an automatic rifle for later use. It seems to be an axiom with the marines that *anything* is possible, even swallowing a whole firearm and passing it through the digestive system without thoroughly screwing up that system, or the firearm itself.

Following a thorough physical checkup, I was given some marine fatigues with immense black letters painted on the back of the shirt, the legs of the pants, and even on the socks and shoes. The letters were all the same: POW.

The letters, of course, meant *Prisoner of War,* and I guessed that the garb had been held over from Vietnam, or even WWII. Whatever, the clothes were warm and comfortable. I was put into a small windowless cell with a thick metal door, a steel bunk with a quarter of an inch thick mattress, and a single ceiling light that was recessed and covered by heavy wire mesh. A closed-circuit television camera was in one far corner, too high for me to reach.

After a fifteen-minute cooling-off period, three guards and their captain entered the cell. The captain, a short, trunklike hunk of a man with muscles that rippled even when he spoke, read me my rights:

"Mr. Nick Carter, by order of the President, you have been temporarily stripped of all constitutional rights. Until further orders from the President himself, you are to remain incarcerated and under constant guard. Your life will not be threatened, nor will you be mistreated in any way whatsoever. However, I must warn you that any attempt to escape will be dealt with harshly and with maximum force. Any attempt to take your own life . . ."

And so on.

I turned him off then. In that cell, there were perhaps one or two ways for me to take my own life, if I were so inclined. I could batter my head against a steel wall until my skull turned to pulp. Or I could hold my breath until my skin took on the cyanosed pallor of the real Charles Ajax in the D. C. Morgue. Or I could eat all my clothes, POW letters and all, and die of indigestion. Otherwise, I was doomed to stay alive.

The captain and two of his marines left. The third marine stood directly in front of the locked steel door, an automatic weapon held at the ready, a big .45 caliber automatic hanging in a holster at his side. There was something familiar about the marine guard, but I ignored him and his weapons and lay on the thin mattress. When I got too restless, I turned my gaze and attention back on the guard. God, he looked familiar to me.

"I suppose I lucked out and wound up in the no smoking section," I said with a trace of sarcasm.

"You're allowed one cigarette each hour, Mr. Carter," he said, glancing at me. "Want me to call another guard to bring you one?"

"Please. But not just any cigarette. There was a pack of my special brand in my jacket pocket when the FBI guys picked me up. Think you could arrange to have it brought here?"

He almost, but not quite, grinned.

"Sorry, sir, but those have been taken to the lab for checking and analysis."

I sighed. "Yeah, I had a stripped-down M16 in a secret drawer at the bottom of the pack. I can see why they'd want to check and analyze it."

"There's no need for sarcasm, Mr. Carter," the guard said. "Do you want a cigarette or not?"

"If I can't have my own brand," I said, "forget it." I looked at him again, held his eyes with mine. He grinned.

"Yes, sir," he said, practically reading my mind. "You know me, or at least you've seen me before."

"I thought so," I said, sitting up, taking a new interest in my environment. "Don't tell me. Let me guess."

I searched my memory. Yes, it was in 1967. I'd just wrapped up an assignment knocking off a bunch of terrorists and had been picked up in the Mediterranean by an aircraft carrier. Hawk was aboard. I was wounded and in the sick bay.

There was a girl, Raina Missou. I'd trusted her, had saved her life. And she'd saved mine, earlier. But there, on that aircraft carrier, she'd told me how she had to get away, to kill the men who had killed her father. She was a beautiful girl, with lovely golden skin and a melodious voice.

But she was also heading for an American jail, under guard. The guards had missed an automatic pistol when they'd disarmed her. She was going to kill me as I lay in that bed in the sick bay.

I'd taken her by surprise by throwing a tray at her. But she'd have nailed me with the next shot if two big marine guards hadn't dashed in just then. They'd disarmed her, hauled her off screaming and kicking. They'd saved my life.

And this marine guard standing in front of the locked cell door with an automatic rifle and an automatic pistol was one of those two big marines who had rushed in and disarmed Raina Missou.

"I'll be damned," I said, getting up and approaching the guard with my hand outstretched. "Good to see you again."

Without thinking, he shook hands with me. I could have ripped his arm out of its socket then. I could have disarmed him, the way he and his buddy had disarmed Raina Missou. I could have gotten the upper hand.

But there was that lousy television camera in the corner of the ceiling. I'd have perhaps two or three seconds to get out that locked door and away before the whole squad of guards, and the stuffy, officious captain came after me. What was needed here was good old-fashioned American guile.

"Good to see you, Mr. Carter. Sorry about all this. I really don't understand why you're under arrest, but I have my orders, you know."

"I know." I released his hand and he immediately clapped it back on his rifle, realizing he'd made a stupid move to take it off. "Say, I didn't get your name back in '67 when you saved my hide from that beautiful lady with the gun."

"It's Anderson, sir. David Anderson."

"From where?"

"Duluth, Minnesota."

"I thought so. There's a certain sound to your

voice. I love that Minnesota accent."

"There are a lot of us Swedes up there."

"Yeah. Well, if you don't mind, I'll take that cigarette now. Any brand will do."

He didn't bother to call another guard. He put down his rifle, once again baring himself to attack, and fished out a pack of Dorals. He lit one for me and passed it over. I could have taken him then. But there was the television camera.

I took a puff, savored the lightness of the tobacco, yearned for one of my Turkish delights, blew out smoke, and sat back on the hard bed.

"You know, David Anderson, somebody is making a big mistake keeping me here. Oh, not you or your captain. You're following orders. But the truth is that there is an imposter, a Russian spy, who has assumed the role of an important American official. He's obviously been feeding the President some wrong data. I'm not asking you to help me. I'm just asking you to listen. When I'm finished, you can do what you like. You can forget what I've said or you can pass along the information. Will you hear me out?"

He grinned and I suddenly fell in love with all the Swedes in Minnesota.

"I'll be happy to, sir, but I don't know what I can do about it."

"Just listen. That's all I ask."

I told the kid everything I had to say. He seemed like a bright young man, a bit above the automaton level. Maybe this would work, maybe it wouldn't.

When I got to the part about seeing the body in the morgue and being convinced that it was the real Charles Ajax, his eyes widened. His mouth quite literally fell open. I knew I'd hit something raw there. When I'd finished the whole yarn, I asked him why he'd responded the way he had to my news about Charles Ajax being dead, an imposter in his place.

"Well, sir," he responded, coming close and letting the automatic rifle fall slack in his hands, "you may or may not know it, but the whole Russian inspection team has been billeted in the officers' quarters here at Belvoir."

"You don't say." I sounded truly shocked, although I'd known it all along, ever since Felicia Starr had told me. I was counting on this guard knowing something—anything—about those team members. "Have you seen any of them?"

"Yes, sir, from a distance, when they arrived. They've been in seclusion since then, but . . ." He stopped, as though divulging more would be a breach of military rule.

"But what? David, don't stop now. You could have an important piece of information there."

He looked troubled. He obviously felt that he was about to become a traitor of some sort. He was obviously from the school of: "A slip of the lip can sink a ship." As much as I wanted him to tell me what was on his mind, I respected the kid for his true patriotism. There's just too little of it around these days.

"Well, sir, I've heard some of the guys talk about how much time Mr. Ajax spends with the Russian inspection team. I don't suppose there's anything wrong with it, but the usual practice when there are visiting inspection teams is that American officials leave them strictly alone. I mean the top officials. Normally, minor state department people or technicians are assigned to be on hand to answer questions. Top officials almost always steer clear."

"And you say Ajax is with them most of the time?"

"Well, not most. But when he isn't at the missile site out west, he's with the team here at Belvoir. Even when he goes to the site, he has a special plane get him back here as quickly as possible. And when he's in Washington, he has a constant convoy running back and forth between his office and Belvoir, just so he can be with the team. Some of the guys thought that was highly unusual."

"And what do you think?"

"I don't know what to think. I mean, until you told me your suspicions, I thought it was unusual. Now, I just don't know."

"Now don't you think it's highly possible that I might be right? Isn't that what you think?"

I knew I had him on the string, that he was putting it together just that way, but I had to pull on the line, make sure. I could see the wheels turning as he pondered my questions that weren't really questions. He drew himself up, set his jaw determinedly, and said:

"Yes, sir, that's exactly what I think."

"And what are we going to do about it?"

"Sir?"

"Look, David Anderson, marine guard who saved my life on an aircraft carrier in the Mediterranean in 1967, you have a chance now to save far more than that. It's obvious that the Charles Ajax who is coming here to be with the Russian inspection team is the Russian spy named Minya Stalin, or Martin Steel. It's obvious that he's been feeding them advance information on what to expect at the site. It's also obvious that the Russians are up to something. I've known it for some time and now you know it. We can't convince anybody else, I'm certain, but we can sure as hell do something to put a crimp in their plans."

"There's no way either of us can do anything," Anderson said, glancing at his watch. "The Russian inspection team leaves in a couple of hours. Mr. Ajax, I've been told, will accompany the team."

"Then, it's important that we call your captain in here and explain the whole . . ."

He was shaking his head, his face gloomy.

"No good, sir. When he sent me in here, he told me you were a spy and a traitor of the highest order. He said you'd concoct any kind of story to get me to let down my guard. He said to kill you if you made the slightest wrong move. I know the captain, sir. He'd be delighted if you made a wrong move and I killed you. He'd recommend me for an award. I don't want to speak ill of the captain, but, well, sir, his mind is funny. Once it closes on something, there's no way to open it."

I sagged on the bunk, out of steam. It was all lost. In two hours, the team would depart by Air Force jet, with Charles Ajax/Martin Steel/Minya Stalin leading them. With the chief of the missile program along, the team would be able to go into those substations and tunnels without any other American officials or technicians along. The phony Ajax would open all the doors, so to speak.

The Russians would be able to do anything they wanted, with total impunity.

The big question was: What did the Russians want to do?

The answer was fairly obvious to me. They

wanted to somehow sabotage the program. It was up to me to find out how they planned to accomplish such sabotage, and to stop them.

But how?

That's why I sagged. There was no way. Even if I subdued this honorable marine guard, the eye of the television camera would reveal my every move.

I'd be shot before I got ten paces away from the cell.

The Russian superspy had won.

As I sat there in defeat, my mind wandered to a little dark smudge on the desert and I saw Rain Allison sitting at his campfire outside his adobe hut.

I really envied that Indian renegade. I'd have traded places with him in a minute.

THIRTEEN

One of life's greatest peculiarities is that the sun seems to shine brightest on the cloudiest of days if everything in life is going well.

Nothing in life was going well for me as I sat in that small, steel-walled call and gazed up at the television camera that was watching my every move.

The treason game would continue. Men like John Pesco and Harold Brookman would continue to sell out America to Russians like Minya Stalin and Natoly Dobrinka.

The missile program would be somehow sabotaged, ruined, scuttled, or God knew what.

I would be slapped hard with murder charges. The President, with strong urging from the phony Charles Ajax, would push for the maximum penalty. The President almost always got what he pushed for and the maximum penalty for killing "patriots" like Allen Pierson and Donald Stanton and Leland Hutchings was, of course, death.

Somehow, Minya Stalin would figure a way to eliminate the wife of the real Charles Ajax. The body in the D. C. Morgue would be buried in a pauper's unmarked grave. The phony Charles Ajax would continue his rape of America without interference.

And Hawk, bless his patriotic hide, would mourn the "fact" that his best agent, N3, Killmaster for AXE, had obviously gone bananas, turned traitor, and played one of the most murderous games of treason since the dawn of the nation. He would be wrong to mourn such a false premise, but he'd never know that he was wrong.

Hawk would never trust any other AXE agent again.

The ramifications of failure were too plentiful and too gruesome to contemplate.

And yet failure lay in front of me, like a long road of broken glass, shards of steel, and quicksand.

Until I had that one clear thought.

When the thought came, it was as though all was going well with life again. An inner sunshine began to pierce the clouds of my mind. I got up and went close to Marine Anderson.

"I know we're on candid camera," I said, jerking a thumb toward the television camera, "but are we also on sound? Can they hear us?"

"No, sir."

"Good. Is this cell soundproof? I mean, if you fired one of your weapons in here, would it be heard by someone outside?"

"It's soundproof. We could set off a bomb in here and . . ."

"But don't you have a way to communicate with someone outside, even your captain?"

He reached in a rear pocket and brought out a tiny quartz walkie-talkie. "I can talk to the men in the television control room with this," he said. "They could summon the captain."

I had everything I needed. Now, it all called for

split-second timing and, for an instant, at least, a very hard heart. I would have to hurt this fine young Marine from Duluth, Minnesota.

"Son," I said, moving to the center of the room, and motioning for him to join me, "I won't ask you to do anything against your Marine Corps oath or your patriotic principles. Even though you share my belief that the missile program is in jeopardy, I have no proof and you can't disobey orders. But you can be taken by surprise."

He had moved up close, partly because I'd motioned him to and partly because I kept lowering my voice. He had to come close to hear what I was saying. He was between me and the television camera.

I did it then. I had to do it.

With one swift movement, I caught him in the groin with my knee. My right hand grabbed his M16 rifle and I let fly a half-dozen rounds of ammo into the ceiling light, shattering the bulb. In the darkness, I found David Anderson's jaw with my fist and knocked him cold. Even as he was falling, I had the little quartz walkie-talkie in my hand. I pressed the button.

"Control room," I said, using that soft, melodic Swedish lilt that Anderson had. "This is Anderson. No trouble here. The light bulb just burned out. I have the prisoner cuffed to the bed. I'll open the door for light. Send maintenance up to replace the bulb."

I released the button and a tinny voice came back: "Roger. He'll be up in five minutes."

I didn't need a fraction of that time.

In thirty seconds flat, I had David Anderson's uniform on and was at the door, inspecting the cor-

ridor. I cradled the marine's rifle in my arms,
jammed his .45 into my hip pocket and dashed
down the corridor toward an *Exit* sign.

Fortunately, the door was unlocked. If it hadn't
been, I would still have gone through it, even if I'd
had to blow it to bits with the marine's weapons.
The fortunate part was the fact that the unlocked
door gave me a few more previous seconds of time
without being detected.

I used that time to skirt around the prison compound and approach the gatehouse. I had the rifle
slung over my shoulder, but kept my hand on the
.45, just in case. A marine inside the gatehouse
looked up from a paperback novel. I had David
Anderson's visored cap low over my eyes. I nodded
and started through the turnstile as though coming
this way were a common occurrence. The guard
put down his book and stood up.

"You with Captain Ordwell's company?"

I was ready to say "yes," but thought perhaps it
could be a trap. This guard might, himself, be with
Captain Ordwell's company or know all the members of the company.

"Not me," I said, laughing. "I've got the best
company commander at the fort."

The guard laughed and I knew I'd guessed right.
Captain Ordwell was obviously the base horse's
ass. He also was obviously the company commander of the guard at the gate.

When I was fifty feet past the turnstile, I began
to look from side to side. Before that, I'd walked
straight ahead, purposefully, as though I knew
where I was going. The plain fact was that I had no
idea where I was in the fort, no idea where the front
gate was. I spotted a walkway down past a building

with a red cross on its side. I guessed the building to be the base hospital and headed that way.

Halfway down the walk, I cut across a street and saw a khaki-colored military bus rumbling along a few blocks down. I tossed the M16 into a clump of bushes. I waited and the bus pulled up to me and stopped. The bus had no passengers. I got on.

"Hope you got a pass to stay out past reveille," the civilian driver said as he closed the doors and pulled away from the curbing with a jar and a jolt. "This is the last bus to Alexandria tonight."

"I got a pass," I said.

He nodded and picked up speed. We took on two more marines at the next stop, then the bus made a hard right and there was the main gate. We breezed through just as sirens far behind began to whine in the warm night air.

The sound of the sirens made me stiffen. The driver cocked his head and the two other marines turned in their seats to look back. To avoid suspicion, I looked back too. Nothing to see, but plenty to hear as loudspeakers began to bark all over the place back there. The bus driver shrugged and picked up speed. We swung onto 395 and streaked northward.

In Alexandria, I lost patience with public transportation. It was too slow. I had to get back to my apartment, tell Felicia Starr the latest findings, gather up new weapons and catch the next plane west. Just thinking of that relatively slow method of travel all the way to Wendover made my teeth go on edge, but I had no choice.

I stole a car in Alexandria and put on an amazing display of speed up U. S. 1 and into the heart of Washington. Even so, more than an hour of precious time had elapsed since I'd clocked David Anderson in that cell and split from the guardhouse of Fort Belvoir.

Felicia was asleep, but she awoke quickly. I brought her up to date while she got into traveling clothes and I changed from the marine uniform into a dull dark suit. I beat her at dressing and called the airlines for reservations to Las Vegas or Denver.

There were no westward flights until 6 A. M. None at all. I could get a flight to Boston, but the next westward flight out of there was even later.

"What will we do, Nick?" Felicia asked. "We've used up all our contacts, and since your escape from Fort Belvoir, there'll be all kinds of people out looking for you."

"I could try once more to convince David Hawk," I said, "but I'm tired of speaking into deaf ears. He has his orders from the President and the President is acting on data from a traitor posing as Charles Ajax. We're strictly on our own."

"I know that," she said. "I've known it from the moment I got involved with you. Maybe that's why I've stuck. Not only do I believe you, but I've always been a sucker for the underdog. You're going to lose, you know."

I looked at her, at that lovely face with its full lips and freckled brow and cheeks.

"That means you lose, too. Want to back out while you still can?"

"No. But this time, you can't leave me out. I stick with you, but you keep me in on every move, no matter how dangerous."

"Do you know what that means?"

"I think so."

"I doubt if you do. Felicia, I'm not just a guy on a government payroll doing a job. I'm a maniac. I'm a highly-trained and highly-skilled killer. Once I set out to do something, I have virtually no scruples. Nothing can stand in my way."

"I figured that."

"I have to stop Charles Ajax from whatever he has in mind," I said, my voice hard and tight. "To do that, I will rob, steal, cheat, maim, and kill—whatever it takes to get the job done. If I learn that I can improve my chances by letting you die, by sacrificing you somewhere along the way, I'll do it without hesitation."

"I know that."

"Do you know why?"

"I have a pretty good idea."

I grinned at her. She had *no* idea. Few people do. I decided to give her a hint, though.

"I don't particularly want to be a fanatic," I said, "but that's just about what I am, when it comes to protecting the interests of my country. I am fully convinced that, in this world, with its awesome weapons, the only winners will be those who are willing to make the ultimate sacrifice to ensure that freedom and individual liberty do not cease to exist. To me, the ultimate sacrifice is not my own life, but the lives of those I hold dear. I don't fight for myself or for my own generation, but for those generations to come. If freedom dies everywhere on this planet, life will continue to worsen until it snuffs itself out from the lack of a will to live. There is too much beauty in life to allow that to happen, to let the deadening influence of mind-controlling masters turn life into a wasteland."

"You're forgetting that men like Minya Stalin are just as dedicated, just as convinced that they're as right as you are. They'll also fight like fanatics."

I shook my head. "No. The Minya Stalins are skilled and trained, but they work for masters who wish to dominate the world. That is a most ignoble desire in this life. I learned something from that Indian out on the desert. I learned that communism and mind-control are ignoble and, as such, cannot make man happy. I'll do what Rain Allison did and quote Plato: 'Man is happiest when ruled by the noble elements in himself.' Freedom is a noble element, domination is the opposite. Freedom is the natural order of things, domination is a man-imposed unnaturalness. It's as simple as that. When a man allows the most noble elements to rule him, he's not only happy, he's more dedicated to his cause."

"And because you're more dedicated than Minya Stalin," she concluded, "you figure to win, even though you're both equally skilled and equally trained."

"I don't figure to win. I may very well lose. Let's just say that, no matter what, I *have* to win. Knowing that gives me the edge."

"You're a very frightening man," she said. "I knew you were dedicated, but I didn't know what ruled you. Now that I know, I'm frightened of you."

"You should be. As I said, I'll even sacrifice you if I have to."

She smiled. "I know. Well, if nothing else, you've just earned a new name."

"What's that?"

"Noble Element. Henceforth, I shall call you said name."

"You do and I may speed up the sacrifice."

She came into my arms then and we stood in that quiet apartment, holding each other, savoring the touch of body against body, wanting to consummate our passion, but having no time to. I pulled away gently. Something was jogging in my memory, an idea was forming.

"Let's go."

"Where?"

"To get some transportation," I said. "We may not be able to get there before Charles Ajax and his Russian stooges, but we can't lag far behind."

I went out the door and Felicia ran after me.

"But there are no commercial flights," she called down the steps. "How in the world . . ."

"Trust me," I called back. "And try to keep up."

In the stolen car, Felicia kept questioning me. Finally, I told her.

"I got the idea from you," I said. "Remember when you told me about Lance Huntington's cottage and how to get there? Remember when you told me that he had two Learjets, one kept in London and one kept in a hanger at National Airport here in Washington?"

"Oh my God," she said. "Surely, you're not thinking of stealing *that?*"

"I'm not going to steal it. I'm going to use what's rightfully mine. Just call me Lance Huntington."

"Nick, can you fly a Learjet?"

"I hope so."

"You mean you don't know if you can?"

"I can fly a Cessna 172," I said as I steered the stolen car down D Street toward an expensive haberdashery, "and I've been in the cockpits of a lot of jet planes. Trust me."

She moaned and muttered something about

being killed by Lance Huntington for getting his cottage blown to bits and now being responsible for the demise of his stateside Learjet.

"Don't worry about Lance," I said, as I stopped a half block away from the haberdashery, and added with a chuckle, "with luck, you won't live to see the rich kid again. But I'm counting heavily on you to tell me more about the romance of Felicia Starr and Lance Huntington. You've flown with him many times, right?"

She smiled. "With or without a plane?"

I frowned. "Right now, I'm only interested in what you can tell me about his toy over at National Airport. Plus a few of his affectations and such. Excuse me a minute. Be right back."

With that, I got out of the car, walked down the street, found a large rock in an alley and crashed it through the window of the expensive haberdashery.

Ten minutes later, with the alarm ringing up and down the otherwise quiet street, I was back in the car, heading out toward National Airport.

In my Pierre Cardin clothes and Gucci shoes.

And working on my haughty, aristocratic accent to use on the mechanics at the hangar where Lance Huntington kept his stateside Learjet.

I had no illusions that this dangerous ploy would work. I just knew that I had to give it my best shot.

FOURTEEN

It was nearly dawn when we passed the Jefferson Memorial and crossed Rochambeau Memorial Bridge, heading back into Virginia and to Washington National Airport. I spotted several police and military patrols, knew they were all looking for me, but I'd pulled another switch on them.

They were looking for a single man in a car stolen in Alexandria, Virginia. A 1982 Pontiac. I'd dumped the Pontiac six blocks from my apartment and had chosen a 1980 Chrysler. I just hoped Mr. Lear had made it as easy to figure out how to fly one of his executive jets as Detroit had made it for thieves to steal their cars.

The Lance Huntington routine went over smoothly, thanks to Felicia's able help. We both pretended we were a bit looped on champagne when Felicia knocked on the door of the quarters at one end of the hangar where playboy Lance's mechanics stayed. I let her do the talking, pretending I was more interested in the sunrise.

The sunrise was an excellent one. I played the playboy role to the hilt, leaping around on the tarmac pretending I was taking photographs. The fact that I had no camera made the gambit all the more believable.

"Tell them to roll it out fast, dahling," I chirruped over my shoulder at Felicia. "I want to be in Indiana before the lovely sun comes up theah."

Felicia's success with the mechanics was predicated on the fact that she'd made a number of middle-of-the-night or dawn trips with Lance Huntington. They knew her by sight. They probably figured she did the flying while her boss sobered up. I tried not to stiffen or show other signs of panic when I heard one of the mechanics say, "I don't know, Miss Starr. We've never seen him quite so looped before. Maybe we ought to call one of the pilots and have him handle the controls."

I whirled, keeping the rising sun between me and the mechanics.

"Deah boy," I said as nastily as any aristocrat in the business. "I am far from looped, as you call it. I don't need Chet or Randy or anyone else to handle those controls. I know them the way I know this lady's—well, suffice it to say, I can handle things from here. Just roll out the Beastie and let's have it done with."

Felicia had coached me well on names, accents, attitudes, and nomenclature during the ride over from the city. The mechanics merely tipped their hats and opened the hangar doors. They rolled the sleek, gleaming white jet out into the dawn. My heart did a couple of flip-flops when I saw the size and sophistication of that beauty. I didn't even know how to start it.

But Felicia had been with Lance enough times on his dippy flights, and I was counting heavily on her. Perhaps a bit too heavily.

The sleepy-eyed mechanics were watching us from the hangar door, so I let the drunk act work for me. I made wild motions in the cockpit as I listened to Felicia's directions.

"Flip that yellow switch up and down three times," she said. "If we get a green light on the screen just below it, the hydraulic system will be functioning. If not, we scrap and let the mechanics try."

She'd already told me that Lance Huntington always started his planes himself, even when he was bombed out of his skull. Turning that task over to the mechanics now would be a sure sign of failure. I couldn't let them get that close to me.

The green light came on. The hydraulic system was functioning. We checked all the systems and controls. Everything worked. Somewhere in the back of my mind, I'd been hoping something wouldn't. The thought of flying this strange animal made my spine tingle, my heart leap.

"Okay," Felicia finally said. "The red buttons to the left of the tachometers are to start the engines. You *do* know what tachometers are, don't you?"

"Sure. I had one in my TR7 before the Washington cops hauled it away."

I started the left engine. It whined and coughed, but soon it was purring smoothly back there. I reached up to hit the second red button.

"Brakes on," she snapped, "or we'll leap clear over the hangar."

I put on the brakes, the engine leaped to life, and we were soon taxiing toward the main runway. For the moment, I knew what I was doing. I flipped on the radio, called the tower, got clearance for takeoff, and lined the sleek mechanism up at the end of the main runway.

My heart was still rattling around in my chest when I hit full throttle on both engines. After that, it might have stopped, for all I knew. I was aware only of an intense pressure in my back, of a long ribbon of macadam whizzing past under my nose, of a terrible roar that might have come from the monsters of my childhood dreams.

There were so many dials, so many controls, so many lights. And so much speed and power.

I closed my eyes and eased back on the yoke, praying all the while.

When the plane was off the ground, I yanked back on the yoke and put her into a steep climb, watching the altimeter and other gauges as we gathered height and speed. At six hundred feet, as ordered by the air controller, I did a ten-degree bank to the left, then climbed to three thousand. There, I did a thirty-degree bank to the right, climbed to eight thousand, hung a twenty-eight-degree turn to the left and set the Omni on a course of two hundred and eighty degrees.

We continued to climb, under radio control, until we reached twenty-eight thousand feet. By the compass, we were heading directly for Seattle, Washington, but the curvature of the earth would correct the setting and bring us, in just over six hours, within a few hundred miles of Wendover, Utah.

The Learjet cruises normally at three hundred and eighty Air Speed Miles. I pushed and went nearly to the max—four hundred and fifty ASM.

"We did it," I said with a grin as we sped westward into the still dark skies. "The Air Force plane taking Charles Ajax and the Russian inspection team will beat us there, but not by much. We have an advantage their plane doesn't have."

"What advantage is that?" She was sitting back

in the copilot's seat, but she was far from relaxed. The little game back there with the mechanics, and the sheer terror of the fast takeoff with a complete novice at the controls had given her quite a case of nerves.

"They have to land at the Air Force Base south of Wendover Range and haul their equipment overland fifty miles to the main inspection site. We can land anywhere we want and taxi right up to the target."

She glanced at me sharply. Her usually wide eyes turned to narrow slits. Her freckles went dark brown.

"You don't mean you're planning to land this delicate piece of machinery on the desert floor, do you?"

"I mean precisely that."

Her face went white, leaving her freckles to stand out, almost three-dimensionally.

"Nick, don't be a fool. This plane has to land at a minimum speed of a hundred and eighty airspeed miles. Even if you don't hit a rock and flip us over and kill us, you'll tear a five million dollar airplane to bits. I mean, pieces will be rattled off this thing so fast we won't even have our seats left when we come to a stop."

"I've walked a lot of that desert," I said, trying to calm her. "I can pick a smooth spot."

"No, Nick. Please. There's a small airfield at Wendover. Put us down there and rent a car."

I thought of the demolished rented car I'd left in that pass south of Wendover. There was only one rental agency in the whole area.

"That's out," I said, and told her why.

"Then steal a car," she pleaded. "Just don't try

to land on the desert. This plane is too delicate, too . . ."

"The lady protests too much," I said, still grinning in spite of the fact that my stomach was already churning at the prospect of hitting a rock, or of seeing the plane disintegrate from the rough landing. "Don't worry so much."

Easy to say. She sighed, heavily. Her ample breasts rose and fell with the sigh.

"Nick, it's one thing to be dedicated—and noble. It's quite another to be crazy."

"I know. Trust me."

The truth was, I didn't trust myself. I'd never landed a jet, never landed *any* plane at more than fifty or sixty miles an hour. We would really be whizzing down into that desert in this handsome, delicate crate. But, short of crashing it into the vehicles of that inspection team going up from Wendover base to the prime missile site, there was no other way to stop what was going to happen.

I just wished I knew for certain what the outcome would be. I had a few fair hunches, none of them very palatable.

One hunch concerned the fact that the team and Martin Steel/Minya Stalin might be on a suicide mission. Once they were inside a tunnel, they'd wait for a missile to come by. By blowing it up in the tunnel, they'd kill themselves, but they'd also play one hell of a lot of havoc with our entire missile program. It would take months to repair the damage and make the system operable again. Meanwhile, Russia would grab a very large edge and, in the interim, perhaps make some thoroughly unreasonable demands on the U. S., or invade another country in the way they'd taken over Afghanistan.

There were other possibilities, but that loomed as the least desirable, and most damaging. I couldn't imagine anything worse.

Little did I know then that Martin Steel/Minya Stalin and his Russian inspectors had a far more extravagant and damaging plan in mind.

All I knew for certain was that I had to stop them from doing *anything* but actually inspecting those sites. And I had to expose Martin Steel, prove that he'd killed Charles Ajax and taken his place. And I had to expose the others—John Pesco, Harold Brookman, and Natoly Dobrinka.

Big chore for a man flying westward in a sleek, delicate Learjet that he really didn't even know how to fly, much less land it on a rough desert floor without destroying the plane, himself, and his beautiful passenger.

"Felicia," I said after a lengthy and painful silence, "listen to me. I know I'm taking a tremendous risk, and asking you to take the same risk. I simply don't know any other way. If we don't beat that team to at least one inspection site before they finish their entire inspection, I may never be able to find out what Martin Steel and his boys are up to. I've been in one of those tunnels. It's impossible for a stranger just to wander in and do damage, but this team will be with a man known by officials there to be the head of the missile program. No questions will be asked. They could do anything they damned well pleased down there and I wouldn't be able to get anyone to listen until it was too late. If you know another way, I'm ready to listen."

She looked at me, without her usual smile. Her large eyes were sad. She swallowed, and I knew it was to put down the lump in her throat.

"We'll do it your way," she said. "I trust you.

And, if we tear up the silly airplane, so what? He's got another one just like it, and enough money to buy a whole fleet of them."

"Not to mention a whole neighborhood of cottages on rivers," I added.

"Amen."

And so it was settled. I would put this slick, speedy device down on the desert floor, or we'd dig a tunnel deep enough for the government to install another wing to its missile system.

"How do we put this critter on automatic pilot?" I asked her.

She moved her hand to the panel of switches above our heads, just above the windscreen, and flipped two switches, then made a slight adjustment of the radio dial. She put that same hand on my hand and gazed into my eyes.

"I want you to know that this won't be the first time I've ever used Lance Huntington's plush couch back there in the passenger section. But it'll be the first time I ever really enjoyed it."

"Remind me to send our rich friend a 'thank you' note."

We went aft to the plush couch, and it was indeed plush. Felicia peeled off her blouse as she walked ahead of me down the narrow aisle. The plane hit a small thermal, gave a neat bounce and Felicia fell back into my arms. My hands went accidentally, but damned near automatically, to her ample breasts. I caught her and kept her from falling. She rubbed her buttocks into my groin and I massaged her heavy breasts through her gleaming white bra. Through the lacy material, I could feel her nipples hardening as lust ran rampant through both our bodies.

I'd long since discarded that smelly poultice and cleaned up my act, so to speak. The wound on my head was covered only by a Band-Aid Felicia had applied before we left my apartment. My side wound had virtually healed. At least there was no more blood oozing between the stitches, and the pain was gone.

"Are you sure you're up to this?" Felicia asked as she turned in my arms and planted those marvelous breasts against my chest.

I pulled her close, and up there, at twenty-eight thousand feet, streaking across the darkening skies of Nebraska, I moved between those long, slender, freckled legs and managed to put aside all else as Felicia and I satisfied each other fully.

Following climax, which came simultaneously and with magnificent force, we lay spent until the plane was nearing the eastern border of Colorado. We had some of Lance Huntington's fine champagne, and by the time we were back in the cockpit preparing for our descent into the dark, forbidding desert floor, we were exhausted but gratified.

"Time to get back to earth," Felicia said as she flipped switches and took the plane off automatic pilot. "I'm shutting down the radio so they can't track us by radio beams. We'd better get below five hundred feet so their radar can't find us."

I'd already been dropping the plane so fast that my ears were popping and also hurting. I knew what had to be done; I just wasn't all that certain of how to do it. Thank God for Felicia—in more ways than one.

Dawn had long since caught up with us by the time we cleared the Salt Lake City area. We could see the town far to the north, a pall of haze above

it from automobile exhaust. I turned the yoke left
and we set a southerly course to bypass the Wendover Range. It took an extra fifteen minutes, but
we circled the range and came up from the south,
over the Pequop Mountains, and took an easterly
heading.

It was too late to catch Minya Stalin and the inspection team at the headquarters site, so I'd decided to strike at familiar territory. I headed for J-
Sector, the one I'd inspected the night I'd piled
sand up beside the fence, driven the rented car to
the top of the pile, and jumped over. I wondered if
that kid with the nasal twang was on duty in the
substation. I strained to recall his name. Roger
Wheaton.

We cruised at five hundred feet and at an airspeed of two hundred and fifty. The desert floor
rushed past below, like a fast conveyor belt hauling
clumps of tumbleweed, cactus, and sandy rocks.
The substation suddenly rose on the horizon and I
turned the yoke to the right to follow the line of the
fence.

"We'll make a pass, check out the terrain, and
land on our return leg," I said to Felicia.

She motioned downward with her thumb. "Action at six o'clock," she said, sounding very much
like an accomplished aviatrix. Which, without
much training, she was.

I tipped the wings and took a look straight
down. There was a line of vehicles on a road leading to the substation. I counted four vans and two
limousines.

"The inspection party," I said. "They've already
been at the main site and are now checking the sub-

stations. Our friendly spy is probably in that lead limousine."

"You think he saw us whiz by them?"

"Probably, but he knows there's no landing strip within thirty miles of here, and he feels confident in the role of Charles Ajax. He probably thinks I'm another Lance Huntington out on a drunken lark."

"You're better than Lance," she said, pressing my hand. "Much better."

I winked, pulled back on the yoke to gain turning-altitude, and went into a three-sixty out over the desert where Rain Allison was probably scratching fleas, talking to his dogs and goats, and looking forward to the next change of seasons.

The Learjet performed marvelously. Hell, it was easier to fly than a Cessna 172. The control responses were immediate and dramatic. But, then, there was a hell of a lot more power propelling us through the sky.

I'd chosen the landing spot. It was alongside the northern fenceline, in the precise area I'd visited when I'd made my unofficial "inspection" of this substation.

I dropped the plane to two hundred feet for the approach. As soon as we saw the fence on our right, I cut the power back and eased forward on the yoke. Felicia watched all my movements, remembering what Lance Huntington had done when he'd landed the plane.

"Down another fifty feet," she said. "We're a tad too high."

Suddenly, the Learjet was far more complex and difficult than the Cessnas I'd flown. There were just too damned many dials and switches and buttons and controls to be concerned about. I thought about killing the afterburners and making a deadstick landing. But jets, I'd been told, had a habit of going into dives in deadstick landings. I thought of the space shuttle and its deadstick landing, but that monster had come in at tremendous speed.

We were down to one-eighty and, though it seemed fast, it was far too slow for a deadstick landing.

When the desert floor was only a few feet below the plane and Felicia had rolled the landing-gear release forward, and we'd heard the tricycle wheels lock into place, I cut power a bit more and eased back on the yoke. At that point, I knew, the plane should begin to float like a feather, like an eagle landing on a rocky peak.

The plane didn't float. It streaked forward, nose down, heading toward that desert floor that suddenly didn't look so flat and smooth.

"Cut power another twenty percent," Felicia said, her voice calm, but anxiety clearly showing through.

The hell with that. I cut power all the way. We were in danger of passing up our target, of landing ten miles beyond and having to walk that ten miles back. I wanted to park this crate within a hundred yards of the pile of sand I'd put beside that fence.

The nose dropped, fast. I pulled the yoke all the way back and waited for the craft to begin to float.

The Learjet was just commencing to float, to drop in like that eagle on the rocky peak, when the wheels hit the ground.

Christ.

We were still descending, dropping too fast.

All hell broke loose inside and outside the plane.

Sand and rocks flew up past the windscreen as though whipped up by a sudden tornado. Not just any tornado, but the granddaddy of all tornadoes.

Inside, Felicia and I were being bounced around like a couple of numbers in a Keno cage. Thanks to our seatbelts, we weren't brained against the ceiling of the cockpit.

The rumble, roar, and rattle of the hard landing built to a fine crescendo. Instruments were shaken loose and began to fly around the place. Glass and Plexiglas cracked and shattered. Loud thumps rippled up and down the fuselage.

And then the landing gear collapsed, or was chewed to bits, and the plane pancaked to the ground like a badly-thrown frisbee. It skipped once, went high in the air, and dropped like a rock to the floor of the desert.

The jolt nearly snapped my neck in two as my head dropped almost to my knees. The only thing that kept my head from hitting my knees was the yoke. It caught me squarely between the eyes and I only vaguely recall the continued screeching, rattling, bumping, clattering, and clanging of the crash landing. I heard Felicia let out a little yelp and then she was silent.

I was silent. Everything was silent.

Through all that silence came the hissing of a valve somewhere as fuel leaked from compression containers onto the desert floor.

And then I was out cold. So was Felicia.

And fuel was leaking. If it caught fire . . .

FIFTEEN

I awoke to an uncanny and almost frightening silence. Felicia was beside me, her lovely head hanging to one side, her auburn hair trailing down over the throttle controls. Behind her was a gaping hole in the side of the plane. I could see the chain link fence and the expanse of empty desert beyond.

There was no hissing of escaping fuel. There was no fire. There was also no sound of Felicia breathing.

I unhooked my seat belt and turned to look back through the plane. Most of it was missing. Great, gaping holes riddled the long body and I could see through those holes, see hunks of metal and other aircraft debris strung along the desert floor in a direct line behind us.

I shook Felicia, convinced that I'd get no response, that she was dead of a broken neck. That ride in had been rougher than anything I'd experienced, short of falling out of a tall tree.

"Felicia. Come on, babe. We have to move it. If they heard this crash, there'll be someone coming out to investigate. Let's go. No time for sleep."

I was keeping my voice light, forcing myself to believe that she was alive, that her neck wasn't bro- •

ken. I lifted her head and peered into that lovely, freckled face. There were no signs of life. I felt my heart start to pound harder, felt an intense depression fill the depths of my soul.

I lifted an eyelid and saw that her pupils were vastly dilated. She was alive, but just barely. Or so it seemed. Then, I became aware that she was struggling for breath, from somewhere deep down in her body. She'd taken a hefty slam in the chest when that plane lurched to a stop. It was possible that her lungs had collapsed.

I wasted no time then. I unhooked her safety belt and pulled her from the cockpit. I laid her out on what was left of the floor back in the plane and knelt beside her. I tilted her head back, forced her jaw forward and put my lips over her open mouth.

I blew the breath of life into her collapsed lungs.

It took three attempts before her eyelids fluttered, her body heaved and shuddered, and she began to breathe on her own. As close to death as she had been, she hadn't lost her sense of humor.

"Do you really think this is the time for kissing and fondling, Noble Element? I thought we came here to stop a spy."

I realized then that I had my hand on her breast, and had it there all the time I'd been giving her mouth-to-mouth resuscitation.

"You damned faker," I said, grinning. "You had the wits scared out of me there."

She grinned back, then took on a somber expression. She shuddered again. "I have the distinct feeling that I wasn't faking, Nick. I thought I'd been knocked out permanently."

I looked around at the ruined plane and thought of the impossible task ahead.

"I'm afraid you got back just in time for the worst."

"I'm ready. Let's get on with it."

Felicia was shaky when we crawled out of the wreck and stood on the desert floor. She was only a tad shakier than I was. But neither of us was badly hurt. I'd taken a bump on the head, alongside the bullet wound Minya Stalin had given me with his AK47, but the wooziness was dissipating rapidly. She'd had the breath knocked out of her, but she was breathing fine now, replenishing the oxygen in her bloodstream.

"I don't know what I'm going to tell Lance," she said, gazing at the plane full of holes and the trail of debris that led out of sight back along the fence.

We set to work gathering up the larger chunks of debris and hauling them to my pile of sand alongside the fence. It was still there, the tire tracks from the rented car still running down one side.

We cleared the fence easily, dropping one at a time into the soft pile of sand on the other side. It all seemed different in the daylight. I seemed to have had a better sense of direction when I'd been here at night. But I found my footprints in the sand, untouched by the wind since my last visit. We followed those footprints and soon came to the line of loose dirt that marked the location of a tunnel.

"We go this way," I said, pointing off toward the left.

Sure enough, that was the way. In ten minutes, we came within sight of the low concrete buildings of the substation. There was the large building that housed the computers and the technician-operators. There was a small building for sleeping quarters, another for the chow hall, another for spare equipment, and a tiny one for obvious reasons. It had a half-moon cut in the door. Unbelievable. In the midst of all this nuclear-age sophistication, a damned outhouse!

The four vans and two limousines were parked a discreet distance from the battered pickup truck and an old Chevrolet that I'd guessed must belong to the technicians on duty at the substation. The inspection team was obviously down below in the tunnels. I'd seen only one tunnel. There were six spreading out from this station. The team hadn't been there long, so there was ample time to check out the vans.

"Why check out the vans?" Felicia asked. "Wouldn't it be better just to take over the substation and keep them down below until we radio for help?"

I'd told Felicia the layout of the station, about the clanking elevator that had taken me far beneath the desert floor to one of the long, wide tunnels—even about the monstrous missile I'd seen rolling along on a caisson that had taken up three sets of tracks.

"Wouldn't work," I said, "unless I can prove that at least one of my hunches is right. If we take over the place and Charles Ajax turns out to be the real Charles Ajax and the inspection team turns out to be made up of legitimate nuclear physicists and technicians, we'd be standing around here with egg on our faces. I need proof and I think the proof is in those vans."

"What proof is that?"

"I don't know. All I know is that every instinct in me says to check out those vans. First, though, I've got to make certain we have the time.

Wouldn't do to be caught in the act. If I'm right in my hunches, we'd be easy bait for the Russians, and there's no military force here to protect us—just a few technicians monitoring the computers."

"How do you plan to do that?"

I grinned and showed her my impressive Treasury Department badge. "I have friends in low, but important places. You hang out behind the outhouse here until I come back. If I don't come back, hotfoot it toward the gate in one of those vehicles. Surely, someone left a key in the ignition."

I didn't wait for her protesting response. I left her blustering behind the outhouse and went directly to the computer control room, hoping that Roger Wheaton would be on duty. The badge would work easily as well with another technician, but I'd become fond of the twangy, towheaded boy from Nebraska.

"Why, Mr. Hunter, I sure didn't expect you back at this time. Your boss and the others are below."

It was Roger Wheaton, all right. His twang made my teeth vibrate.

I put the wallet with the phony badge in my pocket, and stepped inside the concrete control room.

"Good to see you again, Mr. Wheaton," I said. "I missed that melodic voice. Yes, I know Mr. Ajax and the others are below. I'm here to make certain no unauthorized personnel are with them. How long do you think they'll be down below?"

He looked at a digital watch on the wall, then checked with his own wristwatch. Even he didn't trust the computerized equipment wholeheartedly.

"They've been down about twenty minutes. I expect it'll take another ten or fifteen to inspect all the tunnels."

"I'll be gone before then," I said. "Don't want the boss to think I'm up here checking on him. By the way, are the other American officials still with the Russian team?"

It was a hunch, another test. I was forever testing this boy, hoping to draw out information I was unsure of. He passed it.

"Oh, sure. Here's the visitors' manifest, if you want to read it."

He handed me a clipboard and I read the names he'd recorded in a neat hand. Right under the name of Charles Ajax were three names that were not only familiar to me, but gave me great joy. Not only did their presence prove my hunches right—or close to being right—but it would make it easier to wrap this thing up. If I could only find a way now.

The names were: Harold Brookman, the number one aide to the secretary of defense; John Pesco, chief deputy to Charles Ajax; and Natoly Dobrinka, the Russian Embassy contact being fed data by the American traitors. I ran through the names of the Russians. From their titles, I realized that some fairly top dogs had come to join Natoly Dobrinka and Minya Stalin, to make certain they did right. There were about twenty Russians, four of them with impressive titles.

I put a fatherly hand on Roger Wheaton's shoulder. "Listen, son, I have a couple of favors to ask."

"Yes, sir," he said, almost snapping to attention. "Name 'em. I'll do what I can."

"First off, don't tell my boss I was here. I'll see him when all the sites have been inspected. They'll be going to H-Sector next, I presume."

"Yes, sir, then up to I-Sector north of Wendover. I won't tell him you were here. What's the second favor, sir?"

"My car has been overheating and I'm afraid to drive it far until I find out what's wrong. I'd like to borrow your car. In fact," I pulled a wad of bills I'd taken from the cache at my secret apartment, "I'll pay you in advance in case anything happens to it."

He backed away from the money. "Oh, no sir, I couldn't take money from you. My car is the brown Chevrolet. It's in pretty fair shape even if it doesn't look so hot. I won't need it for a couple of days. Meanwhile, my buddies and I will take a look at your car and see if we can fix it. You take my car."

I faked a small protest when he handed me the keys, then left five hundred dollars on a table near the door. I had serious doubts that Roger Wheaton would ever see his brown Chevy again.

"Don't forget," I said, my finger to my lips, "not a word to Mr. Ajax about me being here. He's not to know that the President wants me to keep my eyes on the inspection team."

"The President?" His awe was all over his freckled, wind-burned face.

"Forget I said that," I said, winking. "You understand."

"Yes, sir. I sure do."

I picked up Felicia at the outhouse, and we went quickly to the vans. I opened the door of the first in line.

I could scarcely believe my eyes.

The van was crammed with small wooden crates, clearly marked EXPLOSIVES. One crate was open and I saw the familiar brown oiled paper that is used to wrap plastiques. Plastic TNT. Other boxes held wire and fuses and firing devices. Still other boxes held automatic rifles, three bazookas and dozens of hand grenades. This latter hardware, I presumed, would be used only to fight off anyone who might discover the inspection team's real purpose.

And I knew the real purpose now. The Russians were taking plastic explosives down into the tunnels and planting them in strategic places. But how were they to set them off without killing themselves? And when would they set them off?

The Russians obviously hadn't set off explosives at the headquarters site or at any other substations. That meant only one thing. Timing devices. I searched the van for timers but found none.

I checked the next van and the one after. Each was crammed with plastiques, AK47 rifles, bazookas, grenades, wiring, fuses, and firing devices. In the fourth van, I found the answer.

There were four boxes of highly sophisticated timers, each timer about the size of an ordinary wristwatch without a band. The timers had small magnets that would hold them solidly against the firing devices. But the numbers on the timers made no sense.

Each dial on each timer had numbers in a circle. There was a sweep hand that I imagined clicked off the numbers once the timer was set. But there were ninety-six numbers on each dial. If those numbers corresponded to seconds, the team would hardly have enough time to get out of the tunnel before the plastique blew the place to bits. If they corresponded to minutes, the headquarters site should have been blown to kingdom come an hour ago.

"Good God," I muttered once the truth hit me: The ninety-six numbers pertained to hours. Ninety-six hours amounted to exactly four days. In four days, the inspection team would arrive in Russia.

About the time their plane touched down in Moscow, the headquarters site and all the substations and tunnels in our new missile system would go up in a series of tremendous blasts that would literally shake the sand out of the Great American Desert.

And, if my hunch proved correct, the inspection team, under the guidance of superspy Minya Stalin, posing as Charles Ajax, had figured a way to set off the nuclear warheads in all those roaming missiles.

In that case, more than sand would be shaken up. The whole western half of the United States would literally be blown skyward, to rain down in the form of lethal fallout on the eastern half.

The mere thought of such a hideous plan made me nauseous. What really made me sick was that the plan would never have gotten off the ground if it hadn't been for certain high-placed American government officials playing their grim game of treason with the Russians.

I not only felt justified in the killing of Senator Lou Barker, and of Allen Pierson, Donald Stanton, and Leland Hutchings, I was mentally kicking myself for not going whole hog, for not killing John Pesco and Harold Brookman and Natoly Dobrinka, for not digging deeper into the web of treason to find others who had helped bring this cruel plan so close to fruition.

I no longer suspected Hawk of treason. He and the President—and a host of others—had been hoodwinked and misled by the phony Charles Ajax and the others.

In a sudden burst of clarity, I finally realized why Hawk and the President had kept calling this a sensitive operation.

The Russian inspection team was obviously a demolition squad made up of trained KGB men whose job it was to destroy our entire new missile program.

But the American inspection team, already in Russia, was made up of legitimate American nuclear physicists and technicians whose lives would be in ultimate jeopardy if anything happened to the phony Russian team.

But the big question in my mind was, how much did Hawk or the President suspect the Russians? Did they have any idea as to the depth of their plan? Or were they merely watching from a distance, hoping that the Russians would play the game on the up and up?

The answer was obvious. Hawk and the president didn't really trust the Russians, but felt safe about the inspection team as long as a man of Charles Ajax's caliber was along with them, keeping his eye on their every move. And there were Harold Brookman and John Pesco.

Hawk and the President couldn't know that Brookman and Pesco were traitors, nor that the most trusted government official in the whole missile program was lying on a slab in the D. C. Morgue, that his place had been taken by one of Russia's top spies.

But I knew.

I knew that Minya Stalin had arrived in the U. S. posing as a man named Martin Steel. He'd spotted me tailing him and had set out to eliminate me. Once he'd put me in the hospital, he'd come to my room dressed in clothes identical to David Hawk's, cigar and all. He even knew Hawk's mannerisms, knew that, in my drugged state, I'd be easy to fool.

He'd deliberately set me on a path of suspicion, suspicion of my own boss.

But he hadn't expected my suspicion to lead me anywhere. As Charles Ajax (or as David Hawk) he'd been afraid to kill me in that hospital bed. He'd sent one of his goons to smother me with my own pillow.

By then, Minya Stalin's other goons—members of the phony inspection team—had already kidnapped Charles Ajax and were holding Mrs. Ajax as a kind of willing captive in her own house.

During that period when I had looked for Martin Steel and Charles Ajax, things had been happening behind the scenes. I could only guess at these things, but I'd stake my life on the fact that my guesses would turn out correct.

One guess was that Minya Stalin underwent plastic surgery to make him look as much as possible like Charles Ajax. With the wife safely out of the way and with Ajax's chief deputy, John Pesco, one of the traitors, Minya Stalin had no trouble at all taking over the role of the missile chief.

And, since the inspection of the missile sites in America and Russia were the hottest item going, Charles Ajax was given unusual powers by the President.

It was easy for Minya Stalin, as Charles Ajax, to keep certain items out of the newspapers and off radio and television. Such things as the killing of Senator Lou Barker, of Allen Pierson, Donald Stanton, and Leland Hutchings. It was easy for the Russian goons to kidnap Felicia Starr, the only newspaper person in the world who knew what was really happening to those traitors.

And it was easy to keep the identify of Charles Ajax secret once his body had been fished out of the Potomac River.

It was also easy for Charles Ajax to track my movements, to anticipate my acts and to be there at the critical moment to try to put me in my grave with his trusty AK47 automatic weapon.

The only problem was that I wouldn't readily oblige the Russian as others had wittingly or un-wittingly obliged him.

I still wouldn't.

But there was a burr under my saddle and I had to figure a way to eliminate it before I really did screw up a sensitive operation.

It wouldn't be easy stopping Minya Stalin and his Russian and American stooges. I didn't know if I could, alone—or with me and Felicia together.

But, even if I did, and proved to Hawk and everyone else that Charles Ajax was a Russian spy, revealed how he and his team had wired our missile sites with plastiques, proved that treachery existed, and ultimately saved the day for the missile program, how did I do it and still not place the American team in jeopardy?

Those experts were in the heart of Russia right now. When word reached Moscow that their own "inspection team" had been killed or captured, what would happen to the American physicists and technicians?

The answer to that was also obvious.

The Russians would make boo-coo noise in the world press, hold kangaroo court trials of our legitimate inspection team members and execute the lot.

And what would be our response?

I didn't like to think of it. All I knew was that I had to walk softly, as Teddy Roosevelt had said, but carry a big stick. The most important part of my job now, next to stopping and exposing these Russian demolition experts, was to keep Minya Stalin alive. He alone could prove useful in the delicate operation following what I had to do next.

When I'd told Felicia what I'd found, and told her what I had to do—and she'd studied the unsavory implications of it all—she shook her head in doubt from side to side.

"I wish I could be of more help, Nick, but this is out of my element. You're the expert at intrigue and spy-killing and all that exotic stuff."

"All right, we'll go with my first impulse, one that I had when I first spotted all the bang-bang stuff in the first van."

"And what's that?"

"Blow the bastards to hell with their own toys."

"Right here? You'd destroy the substation and a big section of the tunnels. Not to mention killing the innocent technicians manning . . ."

"Not here. They're going farther west to H-Sector next. After that, they'll swing back around and head north to Wendover and I-Sector. They have to go through a narrow pass. I happen to know that the pass is a great place for an ambush."

"How do you know that?"

I touched the Band-Aid on my forehead, about

three inches above my left eye. It hurt from the bump I'd received in the rough landing. "That's where I got this. Come on. We've no time to waste."

We raided each van, careful not to take enough to arouse suspicion. We loaded two bazookas with accompanying ammo into Roger Wheaton's old brown Chevy. Next came plastique and wiring and fuses and firing devices. I couldn't use the timing devices because I'd need detonation at will. I would rig something up with the fuses and the batteries from a flashlight I found in Wheaton's glove compartment. Next, I snatched two AK47 rifles and extra clips. Then, an idea blooming in my mind, I took one of the four-day timers. Just one.

During the theft, we were out of view of anyone at the computer building, but Roger Wheaton saw us as we drove toward the gate. True to form, he released the lock. The gate swung open and we rumbled through. The Chevy had a peculiar knock in the crankcase, but I couldn't baby the damned thing. We had lots of ground to cover in a short time. We had a tea party to organize. But it all hinged on Roger Wheaton keeping his word, not mentioning me. The Russians mustn't suspect a thing.

We made it to the pass in less than thirty minutes, mainly because I floored the old Chevrolet. I really hoped the five hundred dollars would cover Roger Wheaton's car. It wasn't worth much after my breakneck run to the pass. I think a bearing was in the process of burning itself out when we finally got through the pass and I pulled over behind the butte.

"Okay," I said to Felicia, "let's get to work."

We made some lethal little bombs of the plastic explosives and placed them at intervals along the highway leading to the pass. I was counting on Charles Ajax and the two traitors to come through first, in the lead limousine. Next would come the vans with the wicked "toys," then the following limousine with the Russian bigwigs, including Natoly Dobrinka. I stationed Felicia at the closed end of the pass, on top of the butte where Martin Steel/Minya Stalin had stood when he'd potshot me in the head.

"Let the lead limo pass this point," I said, "and give me a thumbs-up signal when it does. As soon as the first van reaches the last bomb in the row, give me a thumbs down and I'll touch the wires together and hope there's enough juice to blow them all. You stay here with a bazooka and an automatic rifle and work on the limousine with the Russian brass."

"Sounds like I'm getting the lion's share of the work, Mr. Noble Element. What will you be doing all this time?"

"I'll disable the lead limousine, kill whoever's with Minya Stalin, and take him alive. It's as simple as that."

"That's pretty fine tuning," she said. "Why not just kill them all and take no chances."

She was a cool one, this Felicia Starr.

"Because," I said, "without Minya Stalin alive, there's no chance of getting our inspection team out of Russia."

"I don't see how . . ."

"Trust me."

She shrugged.

I started up the highway through the pass, planning to take a station at the top of the butte where Minya Stalin had first fired on me.

"Nick?"

I turned. Felicia was gazing at me, her lips pursed, her freckles standing out in sharp relief.

"Yeah?"

"I'm scared. Supposing it doesn't work. Supposing the bombs don't go off. Supposing . . ."

"It will work," I said. "Just follow my orders and it will work."

I started off again.

"Nick?"

I turned.

She smiled. "Let's knock 'em dead."

"Let's," I said grimly, and went to it.

SIXTEEN

I lay there on top of the butte and picked out the spot in the road where I wanted the limousine bearing Charles Ajax/Martin Steel/Minya Stalin and his Russian stooges to stop. Or where I wanted to stop it.

I didn't want to use the bazooka, even on the radiator. The shells are too damned volatile and unpredictable. The explosion could blow the whole car to shreds, and the spy along with it, if my aim was just a fraction of an inch off.

And the AK47 was also unreliable for short-distance accuracy. I could easily spray the radiator and then kill Brookman and Pesco with the AK47. But I could just as easily allow a stray bullet, or a ricochet off the walls of the pass, to kill the man I needed to keep alive.

I needed to talk with Minya Stalin, eyeball to eyeball. I had a pretty fair idea of just the right words to use on him. He was vital to the plan to get the American nuclear inspection team out of Russia. Until those men were safe, my job was far from over.

But first, the ambush had to work. It all had to come down to one thing: A meeting of minds between two spies, Nick Carter and Minya Stalin.

All the diplomats, and diplomacy, in the world wouldn't work once word got out that an American agent had killed off an entire Russian inspection team invited to our country through the auspices of the United Nations.

The Russian propaganda machine would start cranking the moment word reached the Kremlin. No matter how effective our counter-propaganda, or the truth, the world would believe that the Russians had been cold-bloodedly murdered by one mad-dog American agent. It would not believe that the Russians had come to destroy, had already placed explosives in strategic places in a number of our substations, as well as the headquarters site.

A tangled web of mistrust and lies and treachery would fall on America like a steel net. All of our squirming, our explanations, our protests, would serve only to ensnare us deeper in the net.

I needed Minya Stalin. Him and him alone. Once I had him, I had to use just the right words, or the ultimate aim of this long, grisly game would be lost.

But first, the ambush had to work.

I slid the bazooka and the AK47 aside and nestled Wilhelmina in my palm. I had found my weapons lying neatly outside my prison. It was now up to the trusty, accurate Luger to do the job that I didn't trust the heavier weapons to do. I would have to use her as I'd never used her before.

I heard the throb of internal combustion engines and jerked my head up to look south along the lonely stretch of desert highway. They were coming. One black limousine in the lead, followed by four vans, backed up by another black limousine.

Doubts crept in. Supposing Charles Ajax was in the rear limo? He'd fall victim to one of the bombs, or to the bazooka, or the AK47 wielded by Felicia Starr. Supposing Felicia forgot my instructions on how to use those powerful weapons? Supposing she got nervous and fired too soon? Supposing the bolt jammed on the AK47 and she didn't know how to free it?

Supposing, I thought with the sickest feeling of all, the damned batteries in the flashlight I'd found in Wheaton's car were too weak to carry the load of juice all the way from my position to those homemade bombs on the highway? I'd tried the flashlight and it had worked. But supposing I'd used the last of battery power in the test?

Sweat collected on my palms, made Wilhelmina's grip go slippery, made the two wires in my left hand threaten to short out with the moisture and blow the bombs prematurely. I let go of the wires and the Luger, wiped my hands on my jacket, and glanced at Felicia on the next butte.

She was rigid, the bazooka shoulder-rest in place, her delicate fingers on the trigger guard. She was probably also sweating. After all, she was in the forefront of all this. If the first sally aborted, she'd be the first and ripest target for Russian guns.

It couldn't abort. It couldn't fail.

The throb became louder and was accompanied by the whine of tires on asphalt. The caravan was nearing the pass now. I put the Luger on the top of the rock and took the wires in both my hands. My fingers trembled and I worried that I'd tremble them together and set off the bombs before the right signal came from Felicia.

I got the first signal. Thumb up. The lead limousine had passed the first butte and would come into my line of sight within seconds. Felicia gave the second signal. Thumb down. The vans and trailing limo were in range of the bombs we'd placed along the road.

I touched the wires just as the lead limo came into view. I didn't wait for the boom, or non-boom. I had Wilhelmina in hand and was taking dead aim on the limousine's radiator when it came.

A terrible, thunderous roar ripped through the pass and literally raised me from the ground. I was lying on my belly and the butte actually bucked and slammed me in the stomach. Roar followed roar as the bombs set off the explosives in the vans.

I squeezed off four shots into the limousine's radiator and didn't even hear the sound of the rounds going off. Wilhelmina's bark was stifled by the deafening explosions of plastic TNT, of bazooka ammo, of men screaming.

Her bark was stifled to silence, but not her bite. The first four blasts from the muzzle of that beloved Luger pounded through the grille of the limousine and punctured a gaping hole in the radiator.

Steam was already shooting through the grille when I adjusted my aim and punctured both front tires of the limo.

The big car stopped and a man got out on either side of the front. Ajax's bodyguard and driver, I presumed. This time, Wilhelmina's bark was heard and felt. In the relative quiet of the pass, I squeezed off two well-aimed shots and hit each of the two men squarely between the eyes.

Luck rode with me. Two more men piled out of the rear and I recognized them immediately.

Harold Brookman from the office of the secretary of defense, and John Pesco, chief deputy to Charles Ajax.

With immense relish, I shot the traitors before they were two steps away from the hapless limousine. Minya Stalin, as I'd hoped, was still in the car, probably cringing on the floor of the rear seat.

Then came the PA-PA-PA-POW chatter of an AK47 and I glanced away for an instant to see Felicia Starr bucking from the recoil of the automatic rifle. She was apparently picking off stragglers. I prayed she'd get them all.

In the instant that I looked away, something moved from the rear door of the limousine. I swung Wilhelmina back that way and saw the something dash down the highway just below me, beneath the cliff's overhang.

"Goddamn it," I cursed. "Minya Stalin!"

And it was. The spy had apparently been watching me since the first shots punched through his car's radiator. He'd seen me shoot his bodyguard and driver, and Brookman and Pesco, then had seen me look away, toward Felicia.

Once again, he'd used one of my mistakes to gain an advantage. He'd leaped from the car and dashed across the road to the near side of the pass. He was against the wall of the butte just below me and I had no clear shot at him.

I was inching toward the edge of the cliff when I heard the bark of an automatic pistol and felt the hammerblows of the lead hitting rock just beneath my chest. The sound of those shots, obviously from a Beretta Brigadier, roared like doomsday up and down the pass and through my eardrums.

I snatched up the AK47 and reached out over

the edge of the rock and let fly a whole clip of vicious Russian ammunition. But I knew that I was merely hitting asphalt and rock down there.

The Russian had left that spot as soon as he'd fired the Beretta at me.

I glanced toward the north, toward the end of the pass and saw him. He ran several paces in that familiar swagger, then turned to fire. I lay flat as his accurate laydown of fire whizzed all around me. If I'd moved so much as an inch, I'd have taken a bullet somewhere in my body. I didn't have many unsullied places to take a bullet.

Felicia was still chattering away with the AK47 I'd left her. I hated to leave what was obviously a hot battle, but my main target was getting away. Then, again, Felicia could be killed by the surviving members of that Russian demolition team.

What had I told her back in the apartment in Washington? "If I learn that I can improve my chances by letting you die, by sacrificing you somewhere along the way, I'll do it without hesitation."

And I didn't hesitate. My heart may have remained on that butte, but my body was up and running after the dark-suited figure that was now streaking across the flat desert, heading north toward Wendover.

I scrambled down the path I'd taken up the butte, fell three times, knocked myself half-silly on a boulder, then got up and began running full tilt after Minya Stalin. For a big man, he could move fast, and I was beginning to hurt.

My head throbbed from the bump I'd taken on my wound during the rough landing. My side hurt from stitches being pulled out left and right. Other parts that had taken a beating during the landing

were making their grievances heard. I ignored all
bodily complaints, and put on a burst of speed
that, frankly, I was surprised I had left in me.

The Russian either heard or sensed that I was
gaining on him. He turned and fired off a burst
from the Beretta. I hit the ground. Bullets zipped
past me, so close that I could hear the whine of
their eternal circling arcs. I also heard them hit
rocks behind me.

In a split second, I was up and running again,
gaining once more. I watched the Russian jam in
another clip. I was about to down him with a burst
from Wilhelmina when a warning voice told me
that I might hit him in the wrong place. There was
no time to stop and take aim on a leg or a shoulder.
I couldn't chance hitting him in the head or heart.

I had to talk to the bastard.

I hit the dirt once more as Minya Stalin did what
I'd hoped to be able to do. He stopped, took aim
with both hands and fired off a whole clip from the
Brigadier. Fiery pellets of lead ripped at the ground
around my head as the Russian's deadly aim
moved in on me. I had to distract him.

I fired a burst from the Luger, saw him waver
and then take off running again. I was up and after
him, narrowing the distance between us.

After that last roar from Wilhelmina, there was
virtually no sound out there on the desert, or from
the pass behind me. I felt a pang, wondering if
Felicia had been killed, or if she had polished off
the last of the Russian demolition team and its
bigwig leaders. I toyed with the idea of going back,
to check, to find out if she were alive and needed
help.

But the spy stopped once again, took his firing

stance. I knew I was a goner. I'd been a millisecond too late hitting the ground. It was then that I knew I should have waited for Felicia. Together, we could have finished off the stragglers, then gone after the spy. As a team.

Now, Felicia was probably dead.

I certainly was.

But the Beretta Brigadier is hardly the trusty weapon that the Luger is. When it gets too hot, it jams. Firing off that entire sixteen-round clip had tested the weapon to the maximum and now the Russian was squeezing a dead trigger.

I leveled Wilhelmina at his head and started walking toward him. He stood there, the useless Beretta in his fist, staring at me as I moved inexorably on.

When I was within fifty feet, I saw his face clearly for the first time. A tremor shook my body.

It was Charles Ajax. Except for the eyes. I had seen that face in a hundred newspapers, but I had seen those eyes only twice. Once in file-photos David Hawk had shown me, and once in a newspaper clipping that startled me in a flea-infested adobe hut right out here in this desert.

He was Charles Ajax all right.

He was also Minya Stalin, Russian spy.

"Greetings, Comrade," I said as I stepped up and took the Beretta from his dangling hand. "My compliments to your plastic surgeon."

We were finally eyeball to eyeball again. I stared into those dark, penetrating eyes and could hardly believe that things had come full circle since that day in the elevator. This time, it was different. I was holding the weapon and Martin Steel/Minya Stalin was waiting for his death bullet.

"Who are you?" he asked in a haughty, officious manner.

"You know me," I said. "You've done everything in your power to put out my lights, the way you put out Charles Ajax's lights."

He drew himself up. "*I* am Charles Ajax," he said, still haughty and officious. He reached for a hip pocket, as if to show identification, but I waved his hand away with Wilhelmina. He became even haughtier. "If you're the Russian agent everyone is talking about, I can assure you . . ."

"Oh, cut the shit, Minya," I snarled. "I've come too far and taken too damned many lumps to put up with your little charade any longer. We both know who is Russian and who is not. I saw Charles Ajax on a steel slab in the D. C. Morgue five days after he'd been fished out of the Potomac River. I can hit you with a lot more facts like that, but let's just say for the record that the game is up. We have some talking to do. If I get the right answers, you can go on living. If not . . ."

I shrugged, as if his death meant nothing to me. Actually, it meant a great deal. This man had to live. He had to live so that a whole team of American scientists and technologists in Russia could come home to their country and to their families. But I couldn't put it just that way.

"If you think I'm a Russian spy," he said, retaining the haughty, top-government-official role, "why don't you kill me?"

"Because I need you," I admitted. I saw a slight movement of his sharp eyes, as though he were watching something behind me. I wasn't about to fall for that ploy. True, I was convinced that Felicia was dead back there in the pass. If she were

dead, then at least one of those demolition experts
had survived. He could have been sneaking up behind me. Even as I resisted turning to see if anyone
was behind me, Minya Stalin's hand moved toward
his hip pocket again. I backed off and leveled
Wilhelmina at his head.

He smiled. "Go ahead," he dared. "Shoot."

"It may come to that," I said, gripping the Luger
tightly and wondering if there really was someone
coming up behind me, straining my ears to hear
footsteps in the sand. "First, let's head back to the
pass. I have a friend there who might need help,
then . . ."

"The friend is already here," Felicia's voice rang
out from behind me. I was tremendously relieved.
I almost turned away from Minya Stalin to face
her. Instead, I moved to my right and turned so
that I could see Felicia and still keep the Russian in
Wilhelmina's sights.

"Felicia, thank God you're alive. I thought
they'd killed you."

She was looking at me with a strange expression.
There was something wrong. Her eyes weren't
warm anymore, but they weren't hateful. She
looked frightened, as though she were about to do
something distasteful and dangerous. It was then
that I noticed that she had the AK47 pointed directly at my chest.

"They very nearly did," she said, her voice tight.
"And now I must kill you, Nick Carter. Drop your
gun or I'll do it now."

It was crazy. She couldn't be a traitor. If she
were, why did she kill all those Russians? Why
hadn't she done me in long ago? She'd had numer-
ous chances. Even as my mind fought against be-

lieving that Felicia Starr was a traitor, it was remembering that day on the aircraft carrier in the
Mediterranean, remembering Raina Missou, a
lovely woman I had trusted, who had helped me,
who had saved my life. In the final moment, her
true colors emerged and she had held a gun on me,
ready to fire. Until those marines had come and
hustled her away.

Raina Missou was hardly a traitor, but she had
her own reasons for wanting to kill me.

Felicia Starr couldn't be a traitor, yet she was
standing there with that Russian AK47 in her
hands and had just said: "And now I must kill you,
Nick Carter."

"I don't suppose it will matter in the next
world," I said as I let Wilhelmina drop to the sand,
"but I'd feel better going if you'd explain just why
you're going to kill me."

Minya Stalin started to move closer, to pick up
the Luger, but Felicia aimed the automatic weapon
at him. He stepped back, seeming content to watch
the two of us work out the problem alone.

"I'm a special messenger working for the President," Felicia said. "I've been watching you for
weeks. It was no accident that I was in that Holiday Inn when that Russian spy tried to blow you
away on that elevator."

"Then you're not a journalist? All that crap
about your furniture being hauled out of your
apartment—and you too—and being driven
around the countryside was a hoax? Even Jordan
Alman, the associate editor at the Washington
Times, was stringing me along, pretending you
worked for him but didn't show up for work?"

She shrugged. "That's about the way it was."

There was still something in her eyes. I'd seen that look in a rabbit's eyes when I was a young man and used to go hunting those defenseless little critters. What I'd seen then and what I saw now was one thing, and one thing only.

It was fear.

"What else?" I asked. I was watching Minya Stalin, calculating what his next move might be, calculating how much time it would take me to snatch my Luger from the ground and put it to work. I would have to kill Felicia first, then hope to wound Minya Stalin, keep him alive for what had to come next.

"This man," Felicia said, pointing at the Russian with the AK47, "is Charles Ajax, head of the missile program. No matter what you say, he is and will always be Charles Ajax." Minya Stalin was smiling from ear to ear. "You see, Mr. Nick Carter, Mr. Woods Hunter, Mr. Forest Creature, and Mr. Noble Element, you've been injecting yourself into some truly sensitive operations. As a result, you've put this country into a really bad situation. Single-handedly, you've just murdered a group of Russian nuclear physicists and technicians."

"But you . . ."

"Let me finish," she commanded. There was harshness in her voice. "The only solution now," she said, "is for you to die and for Mr. Ajax here to take the true story back to Washington. That story will be believed in Moscow and our own team will come home safely."

"And what is that story?" I asked, not bothering to hide the bitterness in my voice.

"That one mad-dog American agent took it

upon himself, against all orders, to murder a group of innocent Soviet scientists."

God, I thought, so it was true. I'd suspected my own government of letting it come to that. *One mad-dog American agent.* That's how I'd even viewed myself at times. Yes, it would work. The Russians would buy it. But there were two things wrong with the President's plan.

One, Minya Stalin, a master Russian spy, would remain in the role of Charles Ajax and would head up our own missile defense program.

Two, I would be the sacrificial lamb. I would be killed right here on this crummy desert.

I didn't like the options. Minya Stalin was delighted with them. He beamed happily and stepped forward, between me and Felicia.

"Yes, young lady," he said in his haughty, officious manner, "I am Charles Ajax, chief of the missile program. I don't believe I've had the pleasure of meeting . . ."

He didn't get to finish. I used the opportunity to get in a few lumps of my own. I hit Minya Stalin in the back of the neck with both hands. He lurched forward into Felicia, knocking her down and sending her automatic rifle scudding across the sand. I ignored Felicia now and went strictly after the Russian who was scampering away.

I drew back with my leg and planted a solid kick in the middle of his stomach. He bent low, gagging as though he were going to vomit. I kicked him again, this time on the chin. His head snapped back and I thought for one sickening moment that I'd broken his neck. I hadn't, but damned near. He collapsed in a heap and I was disappointed that he hadn't put up a better fight. He was tougher than that.

Yeah, much tougher. The bastard was faking unconsciousness.

I crawled to him, lifted his head with my left hand and swung a wide haymaker at his jaw. Even as my fist was crashing down, Minya Stalin sensed what was coming. His eyes popped open and he tried to wrench his head out of the line of fire.

Too late.

I hit him so hard that I thought I'd broken all my knuckles. He went out for real this time.

I spun around on my knees and saw Felicia standing there with the AK47 in her hands. It was pointed in my general direction. Her face was grim, unreadable.

Once again, I considered myself a dead man. I was too far away to make a try for the gun. And I was on my knees. She was standing with her feet planted apart.

All it would take was one easy squeeze on the trigger, and a hot volley of copper-sheathed death merchants would be flung across the narrow stretch of desert between us. The lethal charge would riddle my body so viciously at such close range that all the poultices and luck and medical science at humanity's disposal would prove useless.

I was a dead man. At the hands of a woman whom I'd considered truly special.

In that moment, I wished I'd stood still earlier and let Minya Stalin do the job with his Beretta Brigadier.

Death such as this should always come from an enemy, not from one of your own. Especially not from one with whom you'd shared tender moments.

SEVENTEEN

I waited for Felicia to pull the trigger on the powerful Russian-made AK47.

I knew she would do it. She was on orders from the President to make the deaths of the Russian demolition experts seem the result of one mad-dog American agent who had taken it upon himself to murder innocent nuclear physicists and technicians.

She had to kill me. She had no choice. As special messenger from the President, she . . .

She was laughing.

I could hear it coming from deep within her throat. Her eyes flashed with mischief. Her shoulders shook with her laughter and the wicked-looking weapon drooped in her hands, pointing harmlessly at the desert floor.

"What the hell is so funny?" I asked her, a little confused.

Her laughter suddenly changed. It wasn't from anything that might have been funny. It was from hysteria. Laughter with an almost demented sound rang across the desert and echoed down the pass.

I realized that she was having tremendous inner conflicts, that something was going wrong in that beautiful head. I got up and went to her, held her shoulders, shook her to shut off the growing hysteria. She was laughing so loudly that her sides must have begun to ache. Tears rolled from her eyes.

She began to sob and the sobbing was just as uncontrollable as the hysterical laughter had been. I took her into my arms and held her tightly as the sobbing ran its course. Soon, she was calm, sobbing gently, sniffling, wiping her nose and eyes.

"Felicia, tell me what the hell is going on?" I demanded.

She looked up at me and her eyes were soft and full of love. She looked at Minya Stalin, still unconscious on the ground. She looked at the AK47 that she'd dropped at her side. She took in a deep breath, a shuddering, sobbing breath, then let it all out.

"Oh God, Nick," she said, "I didn't think I could pull it off. But I did. It worked beautifully, didn't it?"

I was puzzled as hell. And getting angry that she wasn't helping to dispel the mystery of her actions.

"What the hell are you talking about? What worked? What did you think you couldn't pull off?"

She kissed my lips and pulled away. She pointed toward the unconscious Minya Stalin.

"Look in his rear pocket, on the left side," she said. "I want to see what he has there."

Still puzzled and a bit angry, I went to the unconscious man and yanked up the jacket of his suit. I slapped his left rear pocket and felt the tell-tale bulge of an automatic pistol. There was something familiar about the shape. I pulled it out of the spy's pocket.

It was the Luger I'd had on me when Minya Stalin iced me on that elevator.

It all came together then, what had happened at St. Anthony's Hospital. Minya Stalin, as Charles Ajax, had orchestrated everything. As soon as I'd been taken to the hospital, he and John Pesco and Harold Brookman had slapped a security lid on the place. Hawk had never been notified. There were no guards because Hawk didn't know and because Charles Ajax hadn't wanted guards.

He'd wanted one of his Soviet goons to come in later and put me away. And he'd played that little charade disguised as David Hawk to make me feel safe.

But there was still the puzzle with Felicia. Why had she acted the way she had, threatening to kill me, telling me about being a messenger from the President? I looked up at her, a puzzled expression on my face.

"When I was approaching you two as you were talking," she said, in control of her emotions now, "I saw him try to reach into his pocket, as though to show you some identification. I saw that all your attention was centered there, as though you suspected he had a weapon in his right hip pocket."

"Yeah. That's true. So what?"

"What you didn't see," she said, "was that he was faking you out. He wanted you to keep your eye on his right side. But I saw from a distance that his left hand was moving ever closer to his left rear pocket. I knew you didn't see him and I knew that he'd succeed in getting a weapon, if he had one there, so I decided on one of your dangerous ploys."

"Ploys?"

"Yes. I had to gain his trust, make him think I was in some way on his side. But he'd know I wasn't a Russian spy or an American traitor, so I cooked up that yarn about the President and a story about a mad-dog agent killing . . ."

"You're not a special messenger for the President?"

"Heavens, no. I've never even met the man. Jordan Alman wouldn't let me come near the White House press corps."

My perplexity and confusion weren't melting away as fast as I'd wanted them to. She saw that I was still trying to piece it all together.

"It's really simple, Nick," she offered. "If he'd gone for his weapon, you probably would have had to kill him if he didn't kill you. You said he had to be kept alive, to help in getting our people out of Russia. I still don't know how you plan to do that, but I knew it was important that the spy be kept alive."

"Yeah, go on."

"Even if I could, I wouldn't have shot him to save you, not after you told me he was so important to the job of getting our team out of Russia."

"What do you mean, even if you could? You had the AK47."

She shrugged.

"The damned gun jammed just after I knocked off the last of the Russians back there at the pass. I couldn't have shot a jackrabbit with it."

"You're really something else," I said. "But I still don't understand why you came up with that complicated crap about being a special messenger for the President."

"I heard the spy, how he kept maintaining he

was Charles Ajax. Okay, I thought, I could go along with that. As I crept up, I caught his eye and put my finger to my lips. He thought I was conspiring with him against you. My whole object was to get him to let down his guard, to stop trying to get to his weapon. I had to make him trust me, believe that I was really going to kill you. I'm certain he had a plan in mind to kill me as soon as I killed you."

"But it didn't get that far," I offered, realizing just how dangerous her ploy had been. "When he believed your story, saw that he'd be able to continue as Charles Ajax, he really let down his guard. He'd been playing Ajax so long he actually had begun to believe he *was* Ajax. You'd planned it that way, planned for him to let down his guard long enough for me to take the advantage."

"I'd hoped it would work that way. If it hadn't, I don't know what I'd have done."

I recalled the scene, how it had worked so beautifully. Minya Stalin had stepped between us, a very foolish move. But he'd been acting as Charles Ajax would, stepping up to shake the hand of the woman who'd saved him and his act. It could all have gone wrong, but it hadn't.

And Felicia had pulled it off with a weapon that was jammed and couldn't be fired.

"You are some kind of woman," I said, moving up to take her into my arms again.

She sighed contentedly and I kissed her full lips. I barely heard the scuffling sound behind me. I turned and there was Minya Stalin, the AK47 in his hands. He was crouched, the gun aimed at both of us. He was weaving from that blow to the jaw, but he was alert enough to blow us both away.

If he didn't have a jammed weapon. But he didn't know that.

"All right," he said in a half snarl. "Now the story will go this way. A mad-dog American agent and a misguided American journalist conspired to murder innocent Russian nuclear scientists. I tracked them, got confessions, and then killed them. A plausible story, wouldn't you say, Mr. Carter?"

I nodded. "Very plausible. Why don't you shoot?"

That tipped him. I wanted him to be tipped. He suspected that the gun was useless or I wouldn't have been so eager for him to use it. He moved quickly, going for my trusty old Luger that I'd put on a small rock not far from where he'd lain unconscious.

As his hand closed on the butt of the Luger, my foot clamped over his wrist. He got off three shots into the desert sky. I kicked the gun from his hand.

"And now," I said, "the time for action has ended. It is now time for serious talking, eyeball to eyeball, man to man."

"There is nothing I want to hear from you," he snarled. He was Minya Stalin again. He started off on a tear about capitalist pigs. Felicia and I both chuckled.

"Nick," Felicia said, "I have the feeling that whatever you have to say to this chump, it's going to take some time to get through several layers of thick skull and propaganda. I hate to be a nag, but the day is moving along and the sun is going to be a real scorcher soon. Isn't there some place where we can do what has to be done?"

I thought of Wendover, but I didn't want anyone

even near a telephone to know what had happened out here on the desert, in this narrow pass—not yet. The phony inspection team was already late for its next appointment, but the technicians at I-Sector wouldn't worry. They'd wait patiently—at least for a couple more hours.

That was all the time I needed to give Minya Stalin a few facts of life. If he bought, we'd save our nuclear physicists now in Russia. If he fought, it was a whole new ball game.

"I know just the place," I said. "Come on, let's get the technician's car."

I'd parked Roger Wheaton's Chevy well off the road, behind the right-side butte, where it would be safe. It was. In twenty minutes, we were tooling up to that dirty spot in the desert that Rain Allison, renegade Indian, calls home.

"Hey, welcome back, old buddy," Rain Allison shouted from the door of his adobe hut. His thirteen dogs and seven goats were clustered around him inside and outside the hut. "Figured I'd see you again after all those boom-booms up there in the pass. Looks like you came out ahead, this time."

His sharp blue eyes had already spotted Minya Stalin in the back seat of the Chevy. Stalin was tied and gagged, the latter because we got tired of being called capitalist pigs each time he opened his mouth. Rain's keen eyes had also spotted Felicia Starr and there was dancing and rejoicing in those eyes.

"The man," I said, by way of explanation, "is someone I need to talk to, privately. The woman is, as the hunters say, out of season."

"Read you loud and clear, old buddy," he said. He swept his arm toward the hut. "My house is your house. Use it as you wish."

He nodded to Felicia, allowed his eyes a bit more dancing and rejoicing, then trotted off down toward his garden with his dogs and goats. I pushed Minya Stalin inside the hut. Felicia followed.

"The aroma is familiar," Felicia said, sniffing the foul air.

"It should be. I wore some of it on my head for a few days."

"Ah yes. How could I forget?"

I nestled Minya Stalin on a rugged stool made from a twisted, agony-ridden desert tree, and pulled off his gag. He started off with his capitalist pig crap, so I slapped him across the mouth with the back of my hand. I sat on the edge of Rain Allison's table. Felicia busied herself with Rain's literature, looking through his worn volumes of Plato, gasping over the dirty magazines.

"You listen, Minya Stalin," I said firmly, "and you listen good. I know you're trained to kill and •trained to die. What we want to do here is have a little discussion of fact, not ideologies. I won't even appeal to your so-called logic or your emotions. I'll simply tell you what is to be, and you can accept or reject it. Fair enough?"

"Capitalist pig."

"Commie slave."

We glared at each other for a time. He obviously didn't like what I'd called him anymore than I liked what he'd called me. But, like the angry, naughty children we were, we had to get the name-calling out of our systems. Now, we had to deal with even sillier traits.

"Fact one," I told him, "is that we both want something that's highly important to us. I want to complete this job, get our people back from

Russia, and go on working at what I know best. You want to blow up our missile system and go home a hero, get the Order of Lenin or something. And you want to go on playing roles like Martin Steel and Charles Ajax. Do I have the first set of facts right?"

He was about to call me a name, but he merely nodded.

"Fact two is that we can't both have what we want. Whatever happens, I've disobeyed orders from the highest levels in my country. They won't let me forget it. My future will be forever tainted by that disobedience. As for you, you can't return a hero because we've killed your whole damned demolition team and we'll disarm those bombs you and the team planted in our missile system. How about that? Sound right to you?"

He nodded and spat on the floor, a half-inch from my right loafer.

"Fact three is that you can still return a semi-hero and go on playing your roles. You'll still be Russia's superspy. Somewhere down the road, we'll meet again and one of us will die."

"I can't return home," he said, a bit morosely. "You've made it impossible."

"Very little is impossible, even though most things are difficult. Believe me, it's possible for you to return a hero, or almost one."

He suddenly seemed interested. That vitality that made his eyes distinguishable from all others was back. "How?" he asked.

"I'll get to that," I said. "First, let me see if my guess as to what happens next is accurate. When your team had installed all the plastic bombs at strategic places in our missile system, you were to report that success to a contact at the Russian Embassy in Washington. Right?"

He nodded.

"And that contact would notify Moscow that everything had gone as planned. Right again?"

He nodded.

"After that," I said, "your team would retrace its steps, checking the missile sites again, checking to make sure your bombs hadn't been discovered, taking photographs, then return to Moscow. All that would take about four days. Right?"

He nodded. His interest was lagging. He only wanted to know how he could return to Moscow a hero and I wasn't telling him how.

"What has all this to do with me?" he demanded. "How is it possible for me to return home a hero?"

"It's a simple game of treason," I said. "Want me to show you how to play this latest version?"

His eyes took on the puzzled look again. Felicia, looked up from her reading obviously puzzled, too.

"Go on," Minya Stalin said.

"That brings us to fact four," I continued. "In that phony inspection team, four were high-level officials in your own missile program. It's no sin to admit it, Minya. They're all dead, so it can't make any difference. Am I right?"

"Four were very high officials," he said. "So what?"

"So, according to fact four, two of them were traitors. They were on the payroll of the American government. At the last minute, they betrayed you, led the entire team into a trap, and got themselves killed. Within twenty-four hours, I can guarantee that all the essential documents of this treachery are recorded in Washington. If the Kremlin wants proof of treachery among your trusted team members, we can give it, in spades."

He was silent, thinking. I went on.

"Fact five is the fact that you, alone, suspected these traitors but were hesitant to act in view of their high positions. You alone escaped, hid out for four days in a hut on the desert, then stole a Learjet and fled to Cuba."

"Where would I get a Learjet?"

"I have one. I flew it in here. It's parked right down by the fence alongside J-Sector."

I saw Felicia's shoulders snap back. She knew I was lying to the Russian and it bothered her, upset some noble element within her. But I wasn't lying, only stretching the truth. If I pulled off what I hoped to pull off—a clamp on news of the Russian team's demise until our own team was safely out of Russia—I'd see to it that Minya Stalin had his Learjet to fly to Cuba. I'd see to it if I had to go to London and steal Lance Huntington's other toy.

"We did see a plane from the distance," he said, everything in him now rising to the bait. "It looked damaged."

"Only slightly," I lied. "We have mechanics who can have it shipshape in a matter of hours."

"Where will I hide for four days?"

I spread my hands to indicate the tiny adobe hut of Rain Allison.

"What's wrong with right here?"

He was already scratching fleas. His nose was already rebelling at the stench in the hut. But he had already weighed the alternatives—death as a spy, or a return to his homeland as a failure.

"You think on it," I said, moving toward the

door and motioning for Felicia to follow. Outside, some distance from the hut, she turned to face me.

"You are some man," she said. "But I don't care for the way you lied to that man."

I told her my plan to let him go, to talk Hawk into providing him with a Learjet or to steal Lance Huntington's second aircraft. She looked at me admiringly.

"You really are a noble creature," she said. "You'd actually let that man go, knowing that someday he'd come back to kill you?"

I didn't have the heart to educate Felicia Starr to the many wiles and dirty tricks of agents like me and Minya Stalin. I didn't tell her about the ninety-six-hour timer I'd taken from that van back at J-Sector. Or how I'd plant a bomb aboard the Learjet we would eventually provide the spy with. I was pretty sure Minya Stalin would find the bomb and toss it out before the timer ran out, but I still didn't want Felicia to know that I was going to at least *try* to keep that bastard from reaching Moscow alive. He'd have done the same favor for me.

At any rate, I hadn't kept myself alive all these years by succumbing to the softness that lives in each of us, and more deeply in women in love.

"Nick," she said. "Are you really going to let that spy return to Moscow?"

I looked into those deep blue eyes, at those freckles and full lips, already pursed in worry.

"To tell you the truth, Felicia," I said, looking down toward Rain Allison, no longer envying the renegade Indian his peaceful life, "I'd really have an empty life without men like Minya Stalin around. I'm a dedicated nut, you know."

"I know," she said, a sadness in her voice. "I'd

hoped at one time that I'd be able to turn you into a man dedicated to one woman. But I guess I'll just have to get what I can from you for as long as I can and then go back to the *Times* and be Jordan Alman's whipping girl again." .

I smiled a sad smile and said nothing.

She sighed, clung to me, and watched the happy Indian at play.

My mind was already projecting ahead, at how I'd report all this to Hawk, at how I'd get him to go along with my plan to give Minya Stalin his "freedom."

But I actually had Hawk over a barrel for once.

Half an hour later, Minya Stalin was still considering my offer. I was beginning to sweat a bit. If he didn't agree, if he didn't establish contact with his Washington man and tell him that all was well at the missile site, I'd naturally kill the bastard and try some other way to save our team in Russia.

Just when I was losing patience with the spy, he called out. I was standing with Felicia outside the hut. Rain Allison had disappeared, leaving his dogs and goats in a pen down past the well. I went in and Minya Stalin was glaring at me with those penetrating eyes.

"I agree to your plan," he said. "You must know, though, that I'll come back soon and kill you."

"You can try. It *is* a free country, you know."

I put the spy in Roger Wheaton's battered and clanking Chevy, said a long goodbye to Felicia and started off across the desert. At the end of Rain Allison's lane there was a small creek running up through a section of low, rocky buttes. Rain was up there taking a bath in a pool of tepid water.

By the time I got back, I knew he'd have put his charm to work on Felicia Starr.

In Wendover, I sandwiched Minya Steel into the phone booth with me and called Hawk. The spy wouldn't agree to cooperate or to make the vital contact buying us time until I got certain promises guaranteed by our government. Hawk was on the line within fifteen seconds after I reached AXE control.

"N3, where the hell are you?"

I told him. No sense in lying any longer.

"I should have known," he wailed. "I just got a call from the President. Some nut crash-landed a plane near the J-Sector site, and he got a report that the Russian inspection team didn't show up at I-Sector north of Wendover. Do you know what happened to them?"

I took a deep breath and prepared to give the man a long and complicated report on all that had happened. But first things first.

"To start with, Sir," I said, winking at the unhappy Minya Stalin, "I'll need a Learjet plane that the government must pay for and never expect to see again. Next . . ."

Hawk was already howling his protests. But, as I said, I had him over a barrel.

He'd come through. He always has.

FROM THE NICK CARTER

KILLMASTER SERIES

☐ **TEMPLE OF FEAR**	80215-X	$1.75
☐ **THE NICHOVEV PLOT**	57435-1	$1.75
☐ **TIME CLOCK OF DEATH**	81025-X	$1.75
☐ **UNDER THE WALL**	84499-6	$1.75
☐ **THE PEMEX CHART**	65858-X	$1.95
☐ **SIGN OF THE PRAYER SHAWL**	76355-3	$1.75
☐ **THUNDERSTRUCK IN SYRIA**	80860-3	$1.95
☐ **THE MAN WHO SOLD DEATH**	51921-0	$1.75
☐ **THE SUICIDE SEAT**	79077-1	$2.25
☐ **SAFARI OF SPIES**	75330-2	$1.95
☐ **TURKISH BLOODBATH**	82726-8	$2.25
☐ **WAR FROM THE CLOUDS**	87192-5	$2.25
☐ **THE JUDAS SPY**	41295-5	$1.75

ACE CHARTER BOOKS
P.O. Box 400, Kirkwood, N.Y. 13795

N-01

Please send me the titles checked above. I enclose _____ .
Include 75¢ for postage and handling if one book is ordered; 50¢ per
book for two to five. If six or more are ordered, postage is free. Califor-
nia, Illinois, New York and Tennessee residents please add sales tax.

NAME_____

ADDRESS_____

CITY_____STATE_____ZIP_____

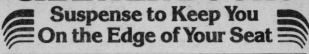